Mr
Nobody's Eyes

Mr
Nobody's Eyes

MICHAEL MORPURGO

EGMONT

For Anthony, Sue, Alexander, Christopher and Nicholas.

EGMONT

We bring stories to life

First published in Great Britain in 1989 by Heinemann Young Books
This edition published 2012 by Egmont UK Limited
The Yellow Building, 1 Nicholas Road, London W11 4AN
Text copyright © 1989 Michael Morpurgo
Cover photographs copyright © 2006 Getty Images

The moral rights of the author have been asserted

ISBN 978 0 6035 6836 7

A CIP catalogue record for this title is available from the British Library

Printed and bound in Great Britain by the CPI Group

55241/1

EGMONT LUCKY COIN

Our story began over a century ago, when seventeen-year-old Egmont Harald Petersen found a coin in the street.

He was on his way to buy a flyswatter, a small hand-operated printing machine that he then set up in his tiny apartment.

The coin brought him such good luck that today Egmont has offices in over 30 countries around the world. And that lucky coin is still kept at the company's head offices in Denmark.

Acknowledgements

My thanks to Nancy and Paul Brinkman, of Ploegsma Amsterdam; and also to Rene te Boekhorst, of the University of Utrecht, for all their help and generous hospitality during the research for this book.

Thanks too to Donal MacIntyre and Sebastian Morpurgo.

CHAPTER ONE

HARRY WAS ALONE WITH HIS THOUGHTS. THERE may have been over two hundred children with him in the playground, but he was quite alone. Maybe it would be today, maybe tomorrow – unless of course something went wrong, and something still could go wrong. Harry knew it was wicked even to think of that let alone to hope for it. But he could not stop himself. He was hoping for it hard.

'We need a goalie!' Peter Barker was bellowing at him from across the playground. Harry turned away. Peter Barker sat next to him in the choir at St Cuthbert's and swapped Turf cigarette cards with him (the ones with the big-headed footballers). Father Murphy's sermons ran on a bit on a Sunday morning and the surreptitious exchanges between the folds of the surplices added sinful spice to the dealing: one Tom Finney for one Billy Wright it was, last Sunday.

'Come on, Harry.' Peter was waving him over. 'We've got no one else.' They were all shouting at him now. He had no choice.

The goal he had to defend was twice the width it should have been, between the two uprights of the rusting chainlink fence with the wilderness of the bomb site behind him. It was fair enough, though, because the other goal was every bit as wide, stretching as it did between the two drainpipes on the lavatory block wall. They often chose Harry for goalkeeper – he wasn't good for much else. He knew he wouldn't have much to do, so he leaned back against the fence and slipped easily into his thoughts.

'An evil thought is a sin in itself, Harry.' That was what Father Murphy had told him in Confession. If that were so, and Harry believed most of what Father Murphy told him, then Harry's heap of sins was piling up fast. He must not allow himself to think about it any more. Instead he would think of Bournemouth. He could always banish his miseries by thinking his way back to Bournemouth. He'd done it often enough over the last two years, ever since Bill came to live with them.

*

Bournemouth was the last time Harry had been happy.

He remembered every hour of it, every minute of it. The war had just finished and they did what his mother had always promised they would do as soon as it was over. They took the train from London down to Bournemouth to spend a week by the sea. All his life he'd wanted to see where the trains went to that steamed past the church and under the bridge beyond the allotments. And now, gazing out of the window, he'd seen the steeple and the graveyard flash past before they thundered under the bridge and were away. His mother sat beside him in her best brown suit, serene in the noise and the smoke of the carriage with the soldiers in their great boots and gaiters laughing their way home, the war done with.

'Your old man in the Air Force, is he?' one of them asked noticing the winged brooch Harry's mother always wore on her brown suit.

'He was,' she said and left it at that. The soldiers quietened, looking at each other and wincing at their own awkwardness, and Harry felt that surge of pride as he always did whenever his father was spoken of. He smiled up at his mother and she held his hand and squeezed it. There was no grief left, not after four years, only a sense of shared loss that bound them together.

Harry hardly remembered his father but his photo was on the mantelpiece in the sitting room, the medal lying beside it.

'Fine boy you've got there,' said the soldier, taking a bar of chocolate out of his breast pocket.

'I think so,' said Harry's mother, smiling.

'Do you eat chocolate, son?'

'Ask a silly question,' Harry's mother said, and the carriage laughed again and rocked rhythmically as everyone ate chocolate all the way to Bournemouth.

To a great leaping cheer, Harry's team scored a goal against the lavatory wall, but it was hotly disputed because the goalkeeper said it had hit the guttering above his head. He held up a piece of the gutter as evidence and a long wrangle ensued before the goal was finally allowed.

Harry smiled and thought of Bournemouth, of number twenty-two Seaview Terrace; of Mrs Coleman, the landlady – 'Call me Aunty Ivy,' she had said – and the little room he had shared with his mother. He remembered the stories his mother had read him in bed, the smell of clean sheets, and the sparrows squabbling outside their window. Then there was the day they had built the sandcastle with its ramparts and towers, with its great cuttleshell walls – hundreds of them they had collected – so that it should be forever impregnable against the sea. He could see now the great moat they had engineered and the driftwood plank that served as a drawbridge. He had stood on the drawbridge and watched the sea surge up the beach and into the moat under his feet only to be held at bay by the cuttleshell walls. Then with the darkness falling and the swifts screaming low over the beach, they had planted a flag in the tower and left the beach behind them, their sandcastle an island now but still standing. And then came the two black dogs with wildly whirling tails, cavorting through the shallows. They stopped by the castle to investigate and decided this was just the place to dig. Perhaps it was the only soft sand they could find. No shrieks, no yells could shift them as they dug in the sand with crazed abandon. Within seconds the castle was reduced to a formless pile of sand. 'Perhaps they were after sea rabbits,' Harry's mother said, as they walked home happy with laughter.

Home was Aunty Ivy's white-painted villa with the green balconies all around, where the food always filled your plate to the edges and where there always seemed to be more. 'Haven't you heard of rationing?' Harry's mother asked.

'Rationing, dear? Never heard of it,' laughed Aunty Ivy, and she tapped her nose conspiratorially. 'We have our ways,' she said, 'and that's all I'm saying.'

It was Aunty Ivy that made up the picnic baskets they took with them each day to the sea or to the cliffs. Harry's mother preferred to eat lunch away from the sand of the beach, so they walked the cliffs searching for the right spot. They would spread out the red-checked cloth, feast themselves on sausage rolls and digestive biscuits, and look down at the gulls and fulmars floating below them on the air.

They were on their way back from the beach one evening when his mother stopped to watch the very last of the sun disappear into the sea. 'That's where your father's plane went down, Harry,' she said. 'He's out there somewhere. Still, no one could have a better grave, could they?' She put her arm round him and pulled him close. 'We mustn't ever forget him, Harry.'

'*Harry*!' The cry came in unison, a cry of dismay and anger. Harry never even saw the ball. He heard it crashing against the wire mesh above his head and felt the crumbs of rust fall on his neck as he ducked.

Recriminations were sharp but mercifully brief, because everyone knew there were only a few short minutes left until the end of break. He conjured up Bournemouth again, although he didn't really want to, not any more. It was like a recurring dream that you have to finish even though you know it ends badly.

The day on the pier was the day it all went wrong for Harry. A fierce gale was whipping the beach into angry sand squalls so that no one could stay there for long that morning. The cliffs were shrouded in cloud so they ate their picnic in a bus shelter and then, tucking the cloth back into the basket, they made for the pier. Harry said he wanted to walk all the way to the end, and so they did, hanging onto the rail and to each other to save themselves from being blown across to the other side. They laughed aloud in the wind and the spray as the waves seethed below them and crashed against the pier. They had reached the end and were breathless with the wildness of it all when the cloth from the picnic basket was whipped out by the wind and flew off down the pier wrapping itself around the rails some fifty yards away. Harry went racing after it but someone was there before him. A tall man he was, with glasses. He had the cloth in his hands. 'Not sure you should be out here on your own,' he said as Harry took the cloth from him, and his mother came running up.

'He's not on his own,' said Harry's mother, 'he's with me.'

'Even so I think it's a bit risky, don't you? Here, let me help you.' He took the basket. 'Come on, take an arm each and hang on.'

They did not need his help and Harry knew it; and what was worse, Harry knew his mother knew it, but she took his arm just the same. Harry had no choice. He followed her example and clung to the man's arm all the way back down the shuddering pier as the waves broke over it, showering them with sea-spray so cold that it took the breath from their bodies. In the shelter of a tearoom the man took off his glasses, shook out his coat, and introduced himself. 'I'm Bill Wesley,' he said, holding out his hand to Harry's mother, and she was smiling at him as she took his hand.

In the days that followed Harry hardly saw his mother. It was Aunty Ivy who built sandcastles with him now and pushed him on the swing in the front garden. 'If I'd had a little boy I'd have wanted him to be just like you, pet,' she told him, 'but Mr Coleman and me, we weren't blessed.' Harry wasn't sure what she meant by that. It was Aunty Ivy and not his mother who read bedtime stories to him, kissed him goodnight and tucked him up leaving the door open for the light. He heard her tell his mother one morning out in the passage, 'I'll look after the boy for you, it'll be a treat for me. I've always wanted one of my own, you know. You go and enjoy yourself with your young man. You're only young once.' And so every morning after breakfast Bill Wesley would come, and his mother would say to Harry, 'You don't mind, do you, dear? Aunty Ivy will look after you. I'll be back before bedtime.' But she never was.

On the last day at breakfast his mother said that Billy – she called him 'Billy' now – wanted to take them both on a boat trip. 'He wants to get to know you a bit,' she said. Harry told her he wasn't feeling very well – he was sure she wouldn't go if he wasn't well. But his ruse backfired on him. Aunty Ivy put her warm hand on his forehead and said she thought he might well have a fever coming on and that perhaps he ought not to go out, that she would be quite happy to look after him. So his mother went out with Bill Wesley on the boat without him.

Harry watched them from his bed through Aunty Ivy's binoculars. He watched them out in their bobbing boat until his anger made him cry. Aunty Ivy said she understood.

She cuddled him close and kissed him. 'It'll be all right, pet. I'll take care of you. If you ever need a friend your Aunty Ivy will always be here. Come on, cheer up. She's a pretty woman, your mother. Only natural she'd take up with someone one day. Nice young man he is too – works in a bank, he tells me. A woman doesn't want to stay a widow all her life – believe me, pet. She should get married again. Only natural.'

And that's just what happened only a few months later in St Cuthbert's. They had the reception in the church hall afterwards. Harry was there, lost in the legs of the wedding guests. 'Are you happy for me, Harry?' his mother asked him. She was wearing the brown suit, but the winged brooch wasn't there any more. Harry nodded.

'Doesn't look very happy to me,' said Bill, bending down and ruffling his hair. 'I'll be looking after you both now, Harry.'

'Give us a smile, Harry dear,' his mother said through her tears. Harry smiled, but just to please her. She kissed him and whispered, 'It'll be all right, you'll see.'

But it was not all right. Nothing was ever to be all right after that.

*

'*Harryyyy*!' Harry started out of his dream too late and the ball rolled past his outstretched foot and through a hole in the fence behind him. They were all shouting at him, Peter Barker amongst them. 'What's the matter with you, Harry?' he said, rushing up to him. 'You didn't even try. We just lost and it's all because of you. You'd better fetch the ball, and quick. The bell's going any second.'

There was a system for getting the ball back if it went through or over the fence into the bomb site. Everyone knew it was absolutely forbidden to go in there. Mr Quigley, the headmaster, had told them often enough – the walls were dangerous and there could even be unexploded bombs. Of course no one really believed that. A dozen or more children gathered around the hole in the fence to form a protective screen so that no one could see what was happening from the school windows. 'But why me?' asked Harry.

'You let the goal in, didn't you?' said Peter Barker. There was no answer to that.

'Anyone about?' Harry asked, looking for any lurking teachers on playground duty.

'All clear,' said Peter, turning Harry towards the hole and pushing him downwards.

Harry scrambled through and had just grabbed the

ball when he heard the bell. He turned quickly and was crawling back when he felt his jumper catch on the fence. He looked up and called for someone to help free him. They had all gone, every last one of them, and Miss Hardcastle was striding across the playground towards him, the bell in her hand. Harry felt his jersey tear, and then his trousers, as Miss Hardcastle took him by the shoulder and dragged him back through the hole.

Miss Hardcastle was known to everyone as The Dragon, and with good reason. To get caught by any teacher in the bombsite was bad enough. It usually meant a dressing-down in Mr Quigley's study as well as several hundred lines and a letter to take home; but to get caught by The Dragon was always a deal more painful. She dealt with things herself and in her own special way. When The Dragon hit you she meant to hurt you. Harry knew that only too well as he was marched along the corridor and into the classroom.

They were all sitting there in awed silence, guilty witnesses of what was about to happen. Not one of them dared to look him in the face except Peter, who shrugged his shoulders and apologised with his eyes. Harry dreaded the ritual but he was determined not to show it. He held out his hand, praying fervently it would be the flat of the ruler across the open hand this time.

'How many times have you been told, Harry Hawkins, that the bombsite is out of bounds?' Harry said nothing. It was better that way, over with quicker. You didn't argue with The Dragon, not if you knew what was good for you. 'You *do* know the bombsite is out of bounds, I suppose?'

'Yes, Miss.'

'Then why did you go in there?'

'To fetch the ball, Miss.'

'So you quite deliberately broke a school rule, didn't you?'

'Yes, Miss.' The worst bit was the waiting. Harry's mouth was dry with fear and the backs of his legs were sweating.

'Deliberate defiant disobedience.' The Dragon was working herself into a temper with every word. She grabbed his fingers and turned his hand over, knuckles uppermost. He knew now he had to expect the worst. 'Perhaps this will persuade you to do as you're told in the future.' And she reached for the long ruler from the top of her desk. '*And* there'll be a letter to take back to your father.'

'He's not my father,' Harry said quietly.

'What did you say?'

'He's not my father. My father's dead.'

'Oh yes, of course, I forgot,' and her lips curled with acid sarcasm. 'We all know Harry Hawkins' father, don't we, the great war hero, the great fighter pilot. You've told us often enough, haven't you?'

'He wasn't fighter pilot, Miss. He was a navigator in a bomber and . . .'

'Are you arguing with me?' Her lips were tight with fury. 'Are you?'

'No, Miss.' Harry knew he was stupid to have started it, but he would not let anyone call Bill his father, not even The Dragon. He winced in spite of himself as she tightened her hold on his wrist and pulled his hand out. He saw her tongue gripped between her teeth and watched the ruler swinging upwards. He did not try to pull away. He'd done that before. She just added another stroke every time he'd tried. His fingers curled involuntarily as the ruler came down, sharp edge first. With the hollow crack came the pain shooting all through him. 'Maybe this!' Again the ruler came down, again and then again. 'Maybe this will teach you. And this! And this!' Harry looked at her, his eyes hard with defiance. She dropped his wrist. 'And don't you dare look at me like that, Harry Hawkins, else there'll be more.' But Harry had no choice. His mouth and his eyes were full of tears that he must not let out. To blink would have been to release them. So he glared up at her, his huge eyes pools of dark anger. Miss Hardcastle seemed suddenly troubled and looked away, muttering to Harry to go and sit down and that he must come to pick up his letter from the staffroom before he went home. It was over.

The last thirty minutes of school were spent writing out in loopy writing, 'The quality of mercy is not strained' in their copy books. Harry's hand hurt so much that he could scarcely hold the pencil. He could not see for the tears in his eyes, tears that despite all he could do dropped from time to time onto his copy book. He would wipe them away before they had time to soak into the paper and hope that no one had noticed, but everyone had. It was a strange thing, but after you'd had a beating from The Dragon, everyone was sympathetic but no one came near you, no one said anything. It was as if you'd suddenly caught an infectious disease of some kind. Harry was grateful for it, though. It meant he didn't have to talk to anyone. He knew he'd find it difficult to talk and not to cry. He waited until he was alone in the cloakroom. Then and only then he cried. Holding onto the coat pegs, he cried up against the wall and kicked it until there were no more tears left inside him.

Miss Hardcastle was waiting outside the staff-room for him. 'Haven't got all day,' she said, and she handed him the letter. 'Go straight home now,' she called after him, 'and mind the traffic. It's foggy out there again.' He was surprised by her concern, by the gentleness in her voice, and looked back at her. For just a flicker of a moment as they looked at one another down the corridor Harry found himself almost believing she was trying to tell him she hadn't meant all she had said, all she had done; but then the moment passed and he hated her again. 'Go on, go on,' she called out, 'and mind you give it to your stepfather. I'll be asking him when I see him.' At least she had called him his stepfather. That was something.

He tied his scarf around his mouth as he stepped out into the smog of the playground. He ran out of the school gates and down the road towards the flashing orange beacons by the pedestrian crossing. He flexed his bruised hand inside his glove and blew on his knuckles to ease the hurt of it. And then he thought of the lectures that would be waiting for him when he got home and handed over the letter, the letter that would say how disobedient and defiant he had been. The lectures would not be from his mother, never from her, always from Bill or Bill's mother, Granny Wesley, who had a face like an ancient crow. She was always at home these days. She had come to help Harry's mother out – that was what she said. Harry could see it now. He could hear it now. She'd take one look at his torn jumper and his ripped trousers: 'No tea for you tonight,' she'd say. 'Thoughtless child. How could you, and with your mother in the condition she's in! Thoughtless.' Or it could be worse still. Maybe it had already happened. They'd said it could be any day now. Perhaps it was today. He couldn't go back home and face that, not yet.

He walked on past the Belisha beacons and made for the park. It wasn't far. Maybe there would be a cigarette packet or two in the wastepaper bin by the bench, always a good place, that, for cigarette cards. It was worth a look, he thought.

Harry found the park gates more by luck than anything else. You could hardly see more than a few yards in front of you, the smog was that thick now. Shadows coughing in the gloom passed him by, and cars and buses crawled along the road, but headlights were all you could see of them.

Harry didn't see anyone in the park, not until he reached the bench by the duck pond. Someone was sitting there, a man who seemed to be talking to the ducks perhaps, or to himself. 'Ocky, Ocky. You come out of there, you hear me. It's dirty. Why you always have to find the dirty places, eh?' He spoke with a strong foreign accent and then seemed to give up English and broke into a different language altogether. Harry could see the man better now. He was dressed in a long overcoat with a fur collar and he wore a wide-brimmed black hat. When he sat back laughing on the bench he was shaking his head. Harry moved a little closer. There was something rustling in the wastepaper bin beside the bench, but he still could not make out what it was. 'Ocky! Ocky! I think there's somebody here,' the man whispered, leaning forward and peering through the gloom at Harry. 'You better come out of there, Ocky, before they see you.' A head came up first out of the wastepaper bin, the head of a black monkey with a pink face and large pink ears that stuck out. And then the rest of it came out and scampered along the bench to sit on the man's lap. The monkey had a cigarette packet in one hand and a newspaper in the other, and was looking directly at him. Harry wasn't sure, but it seemed as if the little eyes that stared back at him were flashing yellow.

CHAPTER TWO

'IS THERE SOMEBODY THERE?' THE MAN SAID, AND Harry stepped forward. 'Come closer.' The man beckoned him towards the bench. 'Don't you worry, she won't hurt you.' The monkey squatted stock still on the man's lap, lips pursed, eyes studying Harry as he approached. Harry came as close as he dared. 'Who is it?' the man asked.

'Me,' Harry said, not taking his eyes off the monkey.

'Ah, it's just a bambino.' He sounded relieved. 'I don't see so good in this fog.' The monkey hooted softly. 'She want to make friends with you,' he said, and he laughed. 'But first I got to introduce you. You got a name?'

'Harry Hawkins.'

'Ocky, this is 'Arry 'Awkins. 'Arry 'Awkins, this is

Ocky,' said the man. 'You got a little something for her, have you? She like the fruit, any kind of fruit. And sweets, she like the barley sugar, 'umbugs. Anything you got.'

Harry fished in his coat pocket. 'Haven't got much,' he said, and produced the only thing he had, an old apple core from the apple his mother had given him for school only yesterday. He held it out, but too fast and the monkey screeched and shrunk back, clinging to the man's coat.

''Arry, you got to be more slow,' he said. 'Ocky's a chimpanzee, and chimpanzees they're a bit like you and they're a bit like me. They got to be sure you're a friend before they like you. So, you got to show 'er you like 'er first. What you got there?'

'Apple core.'

'S'good. She like the apples. So you 'old it out, but gently now, and don't look at her in the eyes. She don't like it when people look at 'er in the eyes.' Harry looked deliberately at the waste-paper bin at the end of the bench and offered the apple core, more cautiously this time. He understood then why the chimpanzee's eyes were flashing yellow, because the wastepaper bin was too – it was the light from the Belisha beacons in the road behind him. It must have been a minute before he saw the chimpanzee move and then she only scratched herself on her shoulder with the cigarette packet. She shifted on the man's lap and looked up into his face uttering faint whimpers.

'*Va bene*, Ocky, *va bene*,' said the man and he stroked the chimpanzee on the head. 'It's just a bambino. You take the apple, Ocky. It's a nice one.' A long black arm stretched out slowly towards him – it was longer than Harry expected – and snatched the apple core. She smelt it first and then bit it in half. It didn't last long and she seemed disappointed there was no more. She searched avidly in the man's lap and in her fur for any last bite of apple she might have missed.

'Say thank you, Ocky,' said the man, taking the chimpanzee's hand and holding it out towards Harry. 'Say "*grazie bene*". She got to learn the good manners. You take 'er 'and now, 'Arry. She don't mind, she's your friend now.' The hand felt like soft, cold leather, and it clung now to Harry's bruised hand with a grip that hurt. The strength of it surprised him. Before he knew it and before he had time to feel alarmed the chimpanzee had swung herself up into the crook of his arm and settled there, an arm around his neck. She was breathing into his ear and had taken the cap off his head.

'She's got my cap,' said Harry, trying to control the

fear in his voice. Chuckling, the man on the bench got up and lifted her off him. He handed Harry back his cap.

'She like to play games, don't you Ocky?' he said. 'You're a thief, a terrible thief. That's no way to treat a friend. Now you take me 'ome, Ocky; we got to catch the bus. We got a show tonight, remember.'

'A show?'

'Circus, Blondini's Circus. You never been to the circus before, 'Arry?'

'No,' said Harry.

'So you come, eh? We have all the animals, it's like Noah's Ark. We got the horses, we got the dogs, we got the sea lions, we got the elephants and we got the clowns. We got lots of clowns. You like the clowns 'Arry? But best of all we got Ocky – she's the big star, aren't you Ocky?' The chimpanzee reached out again for Harry's cap but Harry ducked away smartly. 'You come, eh, bambino? I, Signor Blondini, invite you personally to my circus, and you bring along your friends. You got plenty of friends, eh? I got to go now.' He coughed and patted his chest. 'I don't like this fog, is bad for me. You can't see so well in it either, but that don't make no difference to us, does it Ocky? We got each other, eh? We find our way 'ome all right. Look, 'Arry, she's giving you her cigarette packet. Special present from the wastepaper bin. She like you. She like everyone who is nice to her, all of the animals at the circus, too; but not the dogs. She don't like the dogs. I don't know why, but she go crazy when she see the dogs.'

Harry took the offered cigarette packet and then held out his hand slowly. 'Thanks, Ocky,' he said. Ocky reached out and touched his hand gently. Then she smelt his fingers, looking all the while into Harry's eyes, a deep, penetrating stare that forced Harry to look away.

'*Arrivederci*, bambino,' said Signor Blondini lifting his hat. Harry saw then that his hair was silver white. He was a lot older than Harry had imagined from his voice. '*Andiamo*, Ocky, let's go.' Ocky took his hand and they walked away together. The chimpanzee turned to look back at him once over her shoulder and Harry saw that she had a cigarette card in her hand. Then they were swallowed in the dark of the smog. Harry looked down at the cigarette pack in his hand and opened it. It was empty.

When he got home Bill and Granny Wesley were sitting in the kitchen. He took his coat off. His tea was waiting for him on the oven, corned beef hash. He hated corned beef hash and said so.

'Always fussy, aren't you?' she said. 'Spoilt, that's the

trouble with you. There'll be no bread-and-butter pudding until you finish it.'

'Can I see Mum first?' he said.

'The doctor's with her now, Harry,' Bill said. 'You can see her later.'

'I just want to see her, that's all.'

'Later,' said Bill, an edge to his voice. 'I'm not even allowed up there now, no one is. Now eat your tea like Granny says, there's a good lad.' Harry looked from one to the other. Something was wrong, very wrong. For a start there was no lecture about being late. No one had noticed the tear in his trousers, and Granny Wesley hadn't even told him to wash his hands before he ate his tea. Perhaps this was a good time to hand over the letter from Miss Hardcastle, he thought.

'The teacher said I was to give you this,' he said, taking it out of his pocket and pushing it across the table towards Bill.

'What is it?' Bill asked. There were dark, deep rings under his eyes magnified by his glasses.

'Just a letter,' said Harry, shrugging. Bill looked down at the envelope but didn't seem in the slightest bit interested in opening it.

'Eat up, eat up,' said Granny Wesley, clapping her hands. Harry ate in silence, glancing from time to time at Bill who kept taking off his glasses and rubbing his eyes, and then at Granny Wesley who was knitting. She was always knitting, her needles clicking interminably, sometimes in unison with the tick of the kitchen clock.

He was half way through his bread and butter pudding when they heard voices from the room above them. A door shut. Footsteps were coming down the stairs.

Granny Wesley put down her knitting. 'You stay here and you eat every last bit of it, and don't forget your orange juice,' she said as she opened the door into the front hall. Bill went after her, closing the door behind him. The whispering in the front hall was tantalizingly just inaudible. Harry crept to the door and put his ear to the keyhole. He could still hear no better, so he looked instead. The doctor was in his shirtsleeves and braces and was standing at the foot of the stairs. Bill was listening, head lowered, and Granny Wesley was nodding and looking at her watch. After a few moments she turned away and came back towards the kitchen door. Harry scuttled back to the table and bolted down the last of his bread-and-butter pudding. The whispering was louder now and he could just make out what they were saying. It was Bill's voice.

'I don't care what you do with him . . . I want him

out of here . . . for as long as possible.' Then the door opened and Granny Wesley came in alone.

'Can't I see her now?' Harry asked. 'Is she all right?'

'I have a nice surprise for you, young man,' said Granny Wesley. She often called him 'young man' and that made Harry feel very old. 'You and me, we're going out,' she said.

'Why?' said Harry. She'd never taken him out anywhere before.

'Why? Because there's something I want you to see.'

'What?'

'How would you like to go to the circus, young man? I saw the notice on the way back from the shops today. There's elephants, sea lions, clowns. I haven't been to the circus – oooh – since I don't know when, since before the war certainly. Half past six it starts. We can be there in a quarter of an hour if we hurry.'

Harry didn't argue. He had his coat and scarf on in a flash. Bill saw them out. 'Don't worry about your mother, Harry,' he said. 'She'll be all right.'

Harry loved everything about buses, the race up the winding stairs to get to the top before the bus lurched forward, the ping of the bell as the conductor called out, 'Hold very tight please'. He liked the seat at the front, so that he could hang on to the white rail in front of him and steer the bus round the corners. It was only a few stops, but to Harry's great delight it took an age in the smog. Granny Wesley let him give the money to the bus conductor. Harry watched eagerly as he picked out the tickets, punched them and handed them over. 'You can keep them,' said Granny Wesley. She was being unusually kind to him, and for a moment Harry wondered why; but then they were on the pavement and caught up in a flood of people and carried along with them towards the light of a great tent with coloured lights flickering all around and music blaring from loudspeakers. Granny Wesley guided him from behind into a ringside seat and gave him a toffee apple. He tried to bite through the outside of it and failed. He couldn't open his teeth wide enough.

He was still licking at the toffee when the lights went down, the audience hushed and the drums rolled to a crashing crescendo. A spotlight picked out a white horse, neck arched, walking out into the ring, and then behind came another, and then another, and another and another, until the ring was circled with identical horses. Harry was so close to them that he could smell them as they passed by. The sawdust from their feet flew up and landed on his coat. It was too close for comfort for Granny Wesley who held her handkerchief up to her mouth. She was to keep it there all through the performance. Then came the ringmaster, striding out into the ring, resplendent in red-spangled evening jacket and top hat, a whip in his hand. The horses came to a snorting halt and turned inwards towards him, a tail swishing right in front of Harry's face. The loudspeaker whistled and crackled. 'Signor Blondini is proud to present to you this evening his world famous travelling circus.' Trumpets blared raucously and the show began.

Harry could see the ringmaster's face. He expected him to be Signor Blondini but he wasn't, he was sure of that. He was too tall, too young. As each act came and went he looked for Signor Blondini and Ocky, but very soon he became so absorbed in everything he saw, in the colour and the noise of it, that he forgot all about them. There were acrobats on horseback, somersaulting as they rode, jumping from horse to horse. There were sea lions tossing their footballs from tail to nose and twirling them in the air. There were elephants trooping around the ring, trunks entwined with tails, and dogs that danced on their hind legs. There were jugglers, trick cyclists, fire eaters and, in between every act, the clowns. No one on the front row escaped the soapy water. No one really wanted to – except Granny Wesley. Whenever the clowns came by with their buckets she shrank back in her seat. Harry thought she was trying to pretend she wasn't there.

When Ocky did appear at last, Harry was taken completely by surprise. She was leading a white-faced clown into the centre of the ring. Harry nearly called out, he was so excited. The clown took a violin from under his arm and sat down on a white chair. The lights dimmed and he began to play a plaintive ringing tune that silenced at once all the buzz and the laughter in the audience. Ocky sat at his feet and picked at the sand, eating whatever it was that she found there while the clown played on. He was a sad, pathetic figure out there in the centre of the ring, somehow not in keeping with the brash, bombastic spectacle of the circus. Not for him the baggy trousers, the red braces, the outsize shoes and the grotesquely painted faces of the other clowns. He was dressed down to his red knee-length socks in a black costume covered in large yellow and red butterflies. When he played 'The White Cliffs of Dover' the audience joined in humming softly – some singing the words, but never too loud. And then suddenly the lights were up again and the clown-gang was back. They gathered round to mimic the butterfly clown as he played, but he took no notice. They danced idiotically, waltzing together and polka-ing together, tripping over each other; but the butterfly clown ignored them and played on. They picked up their buckets and were about to empty them on the butterfly clown, turning to the audience to ask if they should. 'No! No!' came the shout, and still the violin played on, a new tune now, a different tempo, faster and more rhythmic. Quite suddenly Ocky was on her feet clapping her hands. All the clowns froze where they were for just a moment, and then the butterfly clown began to sway in time to the music as he played. The clowns followed suit, no longer mocking him. They were becoming lost in the music, hypnotised by it. After a minute or two the butterfly clown stopped playing and laid the violin down on the chair behind him. He looked around the laughing audience, pointed to the still swaying clowns and put his finger to his lips to quieten the audience. Then he took several green balls out of his pockets and began to juggle with them expertly. The clowns did the same. They too dipped into their pockets and took out several green balls and they too began to juggle, throwing the balls higher and higher and then lower and lower, and in perfect time with the butterfly clown. When the butterfly clown finished, he put them back in his pocket, but he left one in his mouth. The clowns, mesmerised, did the same. It was the first and only act that Granny Wesley seemed to enjoy, and she laughed freely, a laugh Harry never knew she had in her. Whatever the butterfly clown did, the other clowns had to do, too. They could not help themselves. If he scratched his nose, they did. If he yawned, they did. If he stood on his head, they did. The audience howled for more, longing for the clown-gang to get more of their come-uppance. The butterfly clown bent down and whispered to Ocky, who ran off and fetched a bucket, a red one marked 'OOZE' in big letters. She dragged it back and left it at the butterfly clown's feet. The butterfly clown bent down and whispered something to Ocky who clapped herself enthusiastically and then resumed her sitting position. All this time the clowns were duly following the butterfly clown's every move, bending down and whispering to chimpanzees that weren't there, and fetching their red buckets marked 'OOZE'. And when the butterfly clown picked up the bucket Ocky had brought him, of course the clowns picked up their buckets, too. The butterfly clown, a wide grin on his face now, showed the audience that his bucket was empty. He turned round and round so that everyone could see. Everyone knew what he had in mind now and willed him on to do it. 'Yes! Yes!' they roared. 'Yes! Yes!' He didn't need much persuasion, but he pretended he did until the audience had insisted loudly enough and long enough. Satisfied now that this was really what they wanted, he lifted the bucket up above his head and turned it upside down, and so did all the clowns around him, covering themselves in a white ooze that dribbled over their heads and down their shoulders. As the clowns wiped their faces the audience roared their approval. They stamped and they clapped, Harry as loudly as anyone. Ocky clapped her hands with everyone else, and then led the butterfly clown in a lap of triumph around the circus ring.

As she passed by, Harry called and called to her but to his great disappointment Ocky never even turned to look. Harry gazed up at the face of the butterfly clown and tried to catch his eye, but he seemed to be looking into the far distance almost as if he was in a trance. Harry waved at him but he never waved back. The man sitting next to Harry was shouting as he clapped, 'That's him. That's Mr Nobody, I know it is.'

'I beg your pardon?' said Granny Wesley over Harry's head. The man was shouting louder, clapping all the while and pointing.

'Him, that clown, that's Mr Nobody. I seen him do the very same thing before the war. Famous he is, Mr Nobody.'

'How do you know it's him?' Harry asked.

'Well you always know with the clowns, son. They all of them wear different costumes, different make-up. Like a sort of trademark. No two clowns are ever the same. It's him, I know it is. No one else like him.'

The lap of triumph had become the grand parade, the finale. The horses came by, and the elephants, the acrobats and the dogs; and the clowns still scooping the white ooze off their faces and throwing it into the audience or at each other. In front of them all came Ocky leading Mr Nobody by the hand. They were coming past him again. 'It's him. I'm sure it is. That's Mr Nobody,' cried the man beside Harry, craning forward. 'It *is* you, isn't it, Mr Nobody?' The butterfly clown heard, smiled and nodded, but he hardly turned his head. Then he seemed to stumble in the sawdust and clutched at the ringside to steady himself, his hand gripping the rail right in front of Harry's seat. His hair grew only sparsely on the top of his head, but was long and bushy and red around his ears. Except for that his entire head down to his neck was chalk white. His startlingly red lips, the same colour as his hair, were painted where there were no lips, but the two black moles above and below his mouth looked real enough. As Harry looked at him their eyes met momentarily and

33

Harry could see why he had stumbled. Mr Nobody's eyes were full of dreams. He was like a man walking in his sleep. And then he was gone, the parade was all over, the magic was broken and they were all leaving.

At the bus stop outside there was a long queue and Peter Barker was there. 'Smashing, wasn't it?' he said and Harry nodded. 'Don't you like your toffee apple?' he said. Until then Harry hadn't even realised he still had it. His hand was sticky with toffee down to his wrist. He began to lick his fingers.

'Still hurting, is it?' said Peter Barker.

'What?' said Harry, knowing quite well what he meant, but not wanting Granny Wesley to find out anything about it.

'Your hand,' said Peter Barker deliberately loudly.

'What happened to your hand?' asked Granny Wesley.

'I fell over,' Harry said, 'in the playground. But it's all right now.' He looked darkly at Peter who was about to argue but stopped just in time to avoid getting his shin kicked.

There was a long cold wait until the right bus came. Granny Wesley stamped her feet and grumbled about the buses, and when theirs came at last she complained to the conductor that it wasn't right to keep people waiting on a night like this and that she was in a hurry to get home. The conductor winked at Harry and said he was sorry but there wasn't a lot he could do about the smog, and that seemed to silence Granny Wesley for a bit. She kept looking at her watch, shaking he head and tutting all the way home.

Bill met them at the door smiling broadly. 'I've got a son,' he said, and he hugged Granny Wesley, who began to cry.

'Can I see Mum, then?' Harry said.

'And you've got a little brother, Harry,' said Bill. 'What do you think of that?' Harry wanted neither a brother nor a sister, but if he had to make a choice he'd have preferred a sister.

'Can I see her?'

''Course you can,' said Bill. 'Just for a minute or two. The doctor says we mustn't tire her. She's had a rough time of it you know, Harry. She had us all worried sick, your mother did.'

Harry's mother was propped up on her pillows, her fair hair all around her, like a halo, Harry thought. She smiled weakly at Harry as he came closer. There was a wicker cradle beside the bed. Harry's mother held out her arms to him, and kissed him.

'Did you have a good time dear?' she said. 'Billy said Granny took you to the circus.' Harry peered down at the baby in the cradle. All he could see was a bright pink, wrinkled face and one tiny clenched fist. There was some dark hair which looked a bit wet. The rest of him was hidden under the blankets. Granny Wesley was beside him now, bending over the cradle, wiping her eyes with a handkerchief. 'Isn't he the perfect poppet,' she said. 'He looks just like Bill did when he was born, just the same.'

'What do you think of him, Harry?' asked his mother. 'Isn't he the most beautiful boy you ever saw? Isn't he?' Harry didn't know what to say because he certainly wasn't beautiful, but he didn't want to have to tell his mother that. So he said nothing.

'We're calling him George,' said Bill, 'after my father. Suits him, don't you think?'

'Oh that's wonderful,' said Granny Wesley. 'Wonderful.' And she cried some more.

Harry went over to the bed to sit by his mother. 'Are you better now, Mum?' he asked.

'I'll be fine dear,' she said, and then her face filled suddenly with anxiety. 'Oh, be careful with him!' she cried. Granny Wesley had picked up the baby and was cradling him in her arms.

'Oh, don't you worry, my dear,' she chortled, her crooked finger stroking the baby's chin. 'I've done this before, remember? I know what I'm doing. You can see the Wesley in him. Big forehead. Sign of intelligence.'

'Please put him down, Granny,' Harry's mother begged, her eyes full of tears. 'Please.' Bill and Granny Wesley looked at each other.

'You're tired, dear,' said Bill taking the baby from Granny Wesley and laying it back in the cradle. 'You'd better go now, Harry. Kiss your mother goodnight and then off to bed with you. It's late enough already and you've got school again tomorrow.' Harry wanted to stay with his mother and he knew she would have liked that too but she would not say so. She never seemed to stand up for him these days. 'You'd better go, dear,' she said. 'I'll see you tomorrow.'

Harry lay there on his bed. No one came to say goodnight to him but someone switched off the light in the passage plunging him into the darkness. They knew he liked the light left on, they knew it. He was relieved though that his worst wishes had not come true. He hadn't wanted the baby actually to die, just not to come, that's all; but since the baby hadn't died, since it had come, he wouldn't have to mention his wicked thoughts to Father Murphy at Confession. He said his prayers lying down. He knew he shouldn't, but it was too cold to get out of bed. He prayed for all the usual people and he included little George too because he thought he ought to. He prayed especially that night for Signor Blondini and Ocky and for Mr Nobody, the butterfly clown, but not at all for Miss Hardcastle, definitely not for Miss Hardcastle.

CHAPTER THREE

THE COMING OF LITTLE GEORGE MADE MATTERS AT home worse for Harry, a lot worse. Whereas before he at least had had his mother to turn to, to intervene on his behalf when there was trouble with Bill or Granny Wesley, she was now so completely absorbed with George that she seemed to have little time for him. He wanted to tell her about Signor Blondini, about the circus, about Ocky and Mr Nobody, but she never seemed to have time to listen to him. She was always too busy. George would need feeding or bathing or changing. Nappies would need washing. 'You can hold him if you like,' she'd say, but without even looking at him. 'He is your brother, after all. Don't you want to hold him?' But Harry didn't want anything to do with little George, or 'Georgie' as they called him now.

It wasn't all bad, though. At least there were fewer lectures on manners and cleanliness from Granny Wesley, and Bill never asked any more probing questions about his marks at school. No one seemed that interested in him any more. And that had one main advantage. Harry could spend long hours in his den without anyone missing him at all.

He was practised enough now at getting there unseen. The quickest and the safest way was through the basement room. It was little more than a cellar, really. The key to the basement was kept hanging on a nail inside the broom cupboard under the stairs. There was nothing left down in the basement except a few old carpets and mattresses, and a couple of battered tin trunks. It was a dismal, dank place at any time but worst in winter. The only light came from the small dirty window that looked out at lawn level into the back garden.

A year ago now he had lit a small fire in the grate just to see if the chimney worked. At first the smoke had billowed out into the room but after a time it seemed to be drawn back up the chimney. On closer inspection, though, Harry found that the smoke was not going up the chimney at all, but that it was disappearing through a hole in the brickwork at the back of the fireplace. It was easy enough to climb through. He knew something of what he would find the other side.

The two houses next to his had been bombed out in the war. Harry hadn't been there at the time. At the beginning of the war his mother had taken him to the country to escape the bombing, not that Harry could remember much about it; but he did remember that when they came back there was a great gap where the houses had once been, and two huge wooden supports propping up their house. From the street Harry had often peered through the fence into the jungle of the bombsite – you could watch the butterflies on the nettles and the pigeons nesting in the ruined walls, but like the bombsite at school no one was allowed in. There was a notice in red letters, DANGER, KEEP OUT. FALLING MASONRY; and he had kept out until the day he'd found the hole in the brick wall at the back of the chimney.

Once inside the bombsite Harry found himself in a similar basement room but much of it was open to the sky, except for over the fireplace where there was still some of the ceiling left. Here Harry made his den, and from it he could climb out and explore the bombsite beyond. He couldn't go near the road for fear of being seen but if he stayed in amongst the undergrowth and the rubble he could go quite unnoticed by the outside world.

He furnished his den from the jumble he collected from the bombsite. Two armchairs with the legs missing, a chest of drawers with one drawer left in it, a mirror to put on the tiled mantelpiece, an old carpet he'd dragged through from the basement of his house, a kitchen table, and any amount of cups and plates and knives and forks. He used to be able to get out of the den by climbing up a heap of rubble, but he'd cleared that away. Now if ever he wanted to explore the bombsite he had to use a homemade ladder, but he rarely left his den now. He had it as he wanted it and this was home to him. He could sit in his kingdom in all weathers and do what he liked and no one on this earth knew where he was. He hadn't even told Father Murphy about it.

He kept his collections of cigarette cards in tin boxes in the table drawer along with his marbles and his store of conkers as well. And high up in the wall, so high he had to stand on the kitchen table to reach it, he kept his money in a pencil box hidden in a niche behind a brick – farthings, halfpennies, lots of pennies, threepenny bits and even a shilling or two. Some of it was pocket money he had saved up and the rest were coins he'd found from time to time in the bombsite. On the mantelpiece under the mirror stood the framed photograph of his father standing smiling by his aeroplane, the photograph his mother had once kept on the mantelpiece in the sitting room. But in pride of place over the mirror hung his father's medal. This was his greatest treasure. He polished it almost every day, not just because he wanted the silver to shine, but because he loved to take it down and handle it, to feel the ribbed purple and white ribbon and the solid weight of it as it lay in his hand. *For Courage* it said on the back, and on the front was the King's head. Harry always thought the King looked a bit like his father, but without the moustache.

Harry would sneak into his den whenever he could, whenever he wasn't at school, whenever he wasn't singing in the choir. Almost every evening he'd go there, although in the short winter evenings it was too dark to stay there very long. One of the tin trunks from the basement served both to hide the hole and to use as a door. Whenever he left he would push it up against the hole, climb the basement steps and reappear in the house. If Bill asked him where he'd been he'd just say he'd been out playing. Sometimes there was no need to tell lies.

Since Georgie's birth it was easier than ever to go

undetected in and out of his den. He still had to take care of course, particularly when coming back up. He would always stop and listen at the top of the stairs for a minute or two and then peer through the keyhole before opening the door and creeping out. Once or twice he'd been caught putting the key back in the broom cupboard, but he'd talked his way out of it each time.

Georgie was famous everywhere, it seemed. Father Murphy prayed for him in Mass. He was the only one who made Harry feel good about it all. 'Isn't your mother the lucky lady?' he'd told him after Mass one Sunday. 'Isn't she the lucky one to have another fine boy like yourself coming along. A few more years and we'll have him singing in the choir just like you.' For all his long and incomprehensible sermons Father Murphy had proved to be Harry's only constant friend.

It was different at school. Miss Hardcastle turned Georgie into a weapon she could use against him. She made frequent jokes. They must have been jokes because most of the children laughed at them. 'Let's just hope Georgie won't grow up to be another Harry,' she said; and another time, 'At least your mother'll have one child she can be proud of.' Harry expected no better of Miss Hardcastle so it did not upset him that much.

You could go two ways home from school. The

short way across the main road, or the long way through the park. Harry preferred the park, and since Granny Wesley didn't seem to be looking at her watch any more when he came in for his tea, he'd been going home that way more and more lately. He'd often passed by the bench near the duck pond and thought of Signor Blondini and Ocky but he'd never expected to see them again. Then one darkening afternoon he walked right past them in a dream of his own and would never have seen them at all had Ocky not called out to him, a soft, low hooting at first, that quickly turned to an excited shrieking.

'What's the matter with you, Ocky?' said Signor Blondini.

'Hello,' said Harry.

'Ah, it's you. It's the bambino. It's a funny thing, bambino, but I think Ocky she know you come again one day. I think she want to meet you again. Every day we go for our walk through the park and every day since we meet you she always stop by the bench and she look this way and she look that way like she was looking for you.'

'Perhaps she just likes the wastepaper bin,' said Harry. It was clear from the mess around the bench that Ocky had been ferreting about in it. Ocky had her hand

45

in a crisp packet and kept taking it out and licking her fingers.

'No, there's plenty wastepaper bins everywhere,' said Signor Blondini, and he tapped his head. 'Chimpanzees, they got a memory better than you, better than me. She remember, and she look for you whenever we come here. Did you come to the circus, bambino?'

'Couple of weeks ago,' said Harry, 'but I didn't see you there.'

'Me?' said Signor Blondini. 'I'm too old these days. I'm the boss. I just count the money and take Ocky for a walk every day. She don't like to be shut up all the time. What do you like the best? The sea lions maybe, or maybe the elephants?'

'Mr Nobody,' Harry said. 'I liked it when he played the violin, when the clowns emptied the buckets on their own heads. Good that was.'

'How you know his name?' Signor Blondini seemed surprised.

'The man next to me, he said he'd seen Mr Nobody before. Said he was famous.'

'Is true,' said Signor Blondini. 'Once upon a time Mr Nobody was the best clown in my circus.' Ocky was on her feet now and pulling at Harry's coat. Harry knew what she wanted at once and gave her his cap. She seemed right away to know what to do with it for she put it on the back of her head, sat down again and busied herself with her empty crisp packet, tearing it apart and licking every bit of it. Signor Blondini put his arm around her. 'But this one,' he said, 'she's the best clown we got now. Come, sit down, bambino.' He patted the bench beside him. Harry sat down. 'When I was your age, bambino – what are you, eh? You nine, maybe?'

'Ten,' said Harry.

'Ten, eh? I was maybe ten years old when the circus come to my village, in Italia. And you know what I do? I run away. You want I should tell you what happened to me?' He didn't wait for an answer. Ocky climbed across Signor Blondini and on to Harry's lap. Harry felt a little apprehensive at first but somehow honoured and delighted at the chimpanzee's trust in him.

Harry soon discovered that Signor Blondini was not a modest man. He had been in his time, he said, the greatest trapeze artiste in all of Italy, maybe in all the world. He had been to the United States of America, to Spain, to France. Everywhere they like to see the circus they went to see the great Blondini. And the ladies they liked him and he liked them, maybe too much. It's difficult to choose right when you've got so much choice, he said. He chose wrong. He married the daughter of the circus owner and within a few years the circus was his. 'That's not so bad. Only one problem,' he went on, 'I like the circus better than I like my wife, and she like the lion-tamer better than she like me, so she run off with the lion-tamer and she leave me with the circus. So that's how come I got the circus. That's the story of the life of Blondini.'

All through the story Ocky had been examining Harry's face close to, sniffing his nose and his ears, looking in his hair with her fingers – what for Harry didn't know. Then she'd settled down on his lap again. Harry saw to his disgust that it wasn't only people that picked their noses. In the end it was a dog that broke up their meeting, a growling little terrier that ran up to them baring its teeth. Ocky leapt shrieking from Harry's lap and clung round Signor Blondini's neck. The terrier yapped furiously, his ratty little body shaking with each bark until his amazed owner arrived, clipped him to a lead and dragged him away. Ocky was very reluctant to walk after that but Signor Blondini calmed her down. '*Va bene*,' he said softly, '*va bene*.' And he stroked her head behind her ears. After a while he set her down on her feet and took her hand. '*Va bene*, Ocky. *Va bene*,' he said. 'You take me home now, eh?' He turned to Harry. 'You ever feel you want to run away sometimes, bambino?'

'Yes,' said Harry.

'Well, take it from Signor Blondini, don't do it. It's not worth it. It's a lot of trouble, I'm telling you. I got no family. I got no education. That's no good. But when you're older and you got some education, then you come and see Blondini and he fix you up with a job in the circus if you like that. All right? You say *arrivederci*, Ocky, to the bambino.' But Ocky was still too worried about the dog. She almost dragged Signor Blondini away, looking behind her over her shoulder all the time. Harry watched them until they disappeared into the gathering darkness.

When he got home there was trouble, big trouble. Granny Wesley's voice was steely with anger as she served him his tea. 'Bill will have a thing or two to say to you when he gets in, young man.' His mother was sitting in the chair beside the stove feeding Georgie. Their eyes met. She could do nothing for him, that much he understood. No one would say what the matter was, but Harry had a terrible dread that his den had been discovered and he prayed and prayed over his baked beans that it would not be so. He did not have long to wait before he found out. Bill hardly had his coat off before he began.

'Now see here, Harry,' he said. 'I've had about as much as I can take from you.'

'Not so loud, Billy,' Harry's mother said. 'Georgie's feeding, you'll upset him.'

But Bill paid her no attention. His anger was in full flow, his voice rising all the time. Granny Wesley sat at the table knitting away and nodding at every sentence.

'If there's one thing I can't stand, it's dishonesty, deceit. And this isn't the first time, is it?'

Harry was still trying to work out what Bill was talking about – it could have been a number of things. It could have been the den. Please God, he prayed again, let it be anything, anything at all, but not the den. The tirade was delivered in the usual manner with his forefinger punching the air close to Harry's nose.

'Who do you think I met after I dropped you off at school this morning?' Harry shrugged his shoulders. 'And don't you shrug your shoulders at me. Miss Hardcastle, that's who. And she tells me she gave you a note to bring home a couple of weeks ago. Now I never saw that note, Harry. So what did you do with it, eh? You hid it, didn't you, or you tore it up, perhaps.' At least it wasn't the den. Harry tried to interrupt but it was no good. 'Rank dishonesty,' Bill roared, 'that's what it is. And what have you done? You've broken school rules again haven't you? Caught in the bombsite she said. Not only that but Miss Hardcastle tells me you were insolent too.' He paused for breath.

'I gave it to you,' Harry said quietly.

'You did not.' Bill's voice broke with fury. 'You did no such thing.'

'I did,' said Harry. He looked across at his mother. 'Honest Mum, it was the night I went to the circus, the night Georgie was born.'

'There he goes, lying again,' said Granny Wesley.

'You'll go to your room and you'll stay there for the rest of the evening,' said Bill.

'Billy,' said Harry's mother. 'Don't be too hard on him. It's not been easy for him, you know.'

'Part of the trouble, dear,' said Bill acidly, 'perhaps part of the trouble is that you weren't hard enough on him when he was younger. Perhaps that's why we're having all this trouble now. I'm not going to lay a finger on him. I never have. I'm not like that. You know it and he knows it, but he must know that he cannot escape from the consequences of his actions by lying.' He was calmer by now. 'Finish your tea, Harry, and then go to your room.'

Harry appealed to his mother. She shook her head sadly. 'I don't know what's come over you these days, Harry,' she said. 'Why do you do these things? Why do you say these things? You never used to be like this.' Harry lowered his head and said nothing. His mother sighed.

'Then you'd better do as Billy says, Harry,' she said.

Harry pushed away his plate. 'I'm not lying,' he said, fighting back his tears. 'I gave it to him, I know I did.' And he went out and ran up the stairs. Once in his room he threw himself on his bed and let himself cry – but silently, so that they should not hear him.

His mother came in later to comfort him.

'Billy's only doing what he thinks is good for you, dear,' she said and stroked his hair. Then Georgie began to cry downstairs and she left hurriedly.

Harry found it difficult to say his prayers when he was angry. He said them that night but he didn't mean a word of them.

A fine drizzle was falling on the way to school the next morning. Bill walked in silence beside him. 'Best pull your socks up, lad, before you go in,' he said outside the school gate. 'And you'll keep out of Miss Hardcastle's way if you know what's good for you.' Bill smiled down at him as he straightened his cap. 'I know you think I'm a bit of an ogre, Harry, but it's because I want the best for you. Understand?' Harry didn't understand, but he said he did. It was easier that way.

He did his very best to keep out of Miss Hardcastle's

way, but morning playtime was the ruin of him. They were supposed to go out in the playground but it was still wet outside and a few of the boys had stayed behind in the classroom, Harry amongst them. There were two ways that cigarette cards changed hands: swapping, where you knew what you were getting; and 'dropping', where you didn't. But with dropping, both the rewards and the risks were much greater. Harry didn't play dropping too often because somehow or other it always ended badly. He was drawn into the game partly because he found it difficult to say no, and also because he had a dozen or so duplicate cards he didn't mind losing; and there was always just the chance he could pick up a card that he really wanted.

The game was quite simple. You gathered round in a circle and someone dropped or flicked a card onto the floor. The aim was to drop your card so that it landed on someone else's. If you managed to do that, then you picked up both your card and the one it had fallen on. With a bit of luck you could even land on two cards at the same time. For several minutes everyone played happily enough. Harry had lost one card and gained two; and then it happened. There were a dozen or so cards on the ground when the door suddenly blew open. The draught lifted and moved some of the cards and Harry found one of his cards had been covered and was being claimed. He didn't think that was fair and said so. Everyone got angry very quickly after that. Pushing and shoving turned to fighting. Harry didn't throw the first punch, but the trouble was that he was the only one still lashing out when Miss Hardcastle walked into the classroom behind him.

'Harry Hawkins again,' she said, shaking her head. 'Always Harry Hawkins at the bottom of everything.'

There was only one punishment worse than the edge of the ruler on the back of your hand. This one lasted longer and was one of Miss Hardcastle's special favourites. 'Because of you and only because of you, Harry Hawkins,' she announced, 'the whole class will stay in for afternoon break, and what's more you'll all stay behind for ten minutes at the end of school.' That was bad enough for he knew everyone would blame him and him alone, but worse was to follow. It dawned very slowly on him at first, but it soon became quite clear that he was being 'sent to Coventry' by all the other children in his class. No one would speak to him. No one would even look at him. They simply ignored him. He hated them for it, all of them. After all, they'd been fighting too, hadn't they? It wasn't all his fault. They were blaming him because he'd had the misfortune to be caught, that's all. Harry tried to put a brave face on it and pretend he did not care, but he did. Every rebuff, every cold shoulder made it more difficult to bear, so that by the end of school he was raw with the hurt of it.

Outside there was a pea-souper of a smog again and Harry wandered home through it filled with misery. He found himself sitting on the bench in the park and thinking about the story Signor Blondini had told him, about how he had run away when he was a boy. Things could not be worse than they were now, he was sure of that. He had no real home, not any more; and no friends. School had become a nightmare. He had nothing to lose. He'd run away. Yes, that's what he'd do. That would show them. He'd run away.

He was just working out where he could run to when he heard a dog barking. He couldn't see it yet, but the barking was deep and angry and it was coming his way. Then Ocky came out of the smog running on all fours, a dog close behind her. The dog was as big as it sounded, dwarfing the terrified Ocky. When she saw Harry on the bench she hesitated for only a split second and then leapt onto his lap, climbing up on his shoulders to shriek her defiance at the oncoming dog from behind Harry's head. Harry would have run too, but it was too late. He only had time to stand up before the dog was there, snapping at him in a frenzy, hackles up and snarling. There was only one thing Harry could do. He kicked out wildly and found his mark. The dog yelped and slunk off whining in the direction he had come from.

Ocky was shaking with fear and so was Harry. He had the presence of mind though to remember what Signor Blondini had done. He stroked the top of Ocky's head behind her ears and talked to her softly. '*Va bene*, Ocky. *Va bene*. He's gone now. *Va bene*.' Whether it was his words or the crisp packet he offered her that consoled her Harry wasn't sure, but she was very soon sitting happily beside him on the bench tearing it to pieces.

'What are you doing out here on your own Ocky?' Harry said. 'Where's Signor Blondini?' He walked hand in hand with Ocky up and down the path that ran through the park searching for Signor Blondini. There was no sign of him. He thought then of taking Ocky back to the circus, but he wasn't sure where it was exactly, and anyway he hadn't got the money for the fare. There was only one thing left he could do. 'We'll have to go home, Ocky,' he said. 'I've got just the place for you. You'll like it there. You'll have a room of your own and I'll take you back to Signor Blondini tomorrow.

Honest I will. Anyway he won't mind if I borrow you just for one night, will he?' Harry looked down into Ocky's upturned face and clutched her hand tighter. 'We'll be all right together, Ocky. You and me, we'll be all right.'

CHAPTER FOUR

WITHOUT THE SMOG TO HIDE THEM IT WOULD have been impossible to reach home undiscovered, let alone spirit Ocky into the den. They passed several people, heads bent into the smog, scarves over their noses. If they were seen, then people saw what they thought they saw, two children walking home from school holding hands. If they had been recognised Harry would have had no ready tale to tell, no convincing explanation. He was far too busy trying to work out how he could sneak Ocky in through the front door, down through the basement and into the den beyond. It became more and more apparent to him as he neared home that it would be too much of a risk to take. There was only one other way in. He'd have to climb into the bombsite over the wire. In this dense smog he thought they could probably get away with it without being seen. He'd never climbed it before and he wasn't sure he could. Ocky would have to hang on to his shoulders.

In the event Ocky did no such thing. She was up the wire in a flash and hung there at the top by one arm waiting for Harry to find his first foothold. By the time he did reach the top Ocky was gone and nowhere to be seen. He could hear her rustling through the under-growth. He dared not call out for her but let himself drop down into the bombsite and went after her. Once far enough from the road he ventured a whispered call.

All about him the ruined walls loomed out of the smog. There was no sign of Ocky, not at first; and then part of the brickwork moved high above him and hooted. He knew that wall, the bricks were crumbling at the edges, and he did not want to go up after her. He tried to sweet-talk her down. Ocky squatted, elbows on her knees, one arm clutching her shoulder looking down at him with complete disinterest. Harry tried the '*Va bene*' magic again and again, but it didn't seem to work no matter how often nor how gently he said it. Ocky would just look the other way, scratch herself or pick her nose nonchalantly. There was nothing for it, he would have to go up and fetch her. He put down his satchel and started up. It was easy enough at first but the higher he went the fewer the footholds he found. He stopped from time to time and tried to talk her down, but it was no good. The higher he climbed the higher she climbed, and when Harry at last reached the top she had disappeared completely.

He rested for a while to calm his shaking knees. He was surrounded now entirely by smog. There were no houses, no trees, no walls. He looked down. The bombsite was there below him. He knew it but he could not see it. He called again for Ocky and heard her hooting reply somewhere far below. By now Harry was beginning to wish he had taken her back to the circus in the first place. The journey down was even more precarious, his feet slipping often on the wet bricks. There was one horrible, heart-stopping moment when a brick gave way under his weight and he was left clinging on by his hands and listening to the shower of bricks and cement as they fell into the undergrowth beneath him.

When he finally got down Ocky was there, busily searching in the grass. 'Your idea of a game, I suppose,' said Harry taking her hand in a firm grip. He did not let her go until he'd leant out over the ceiling of his den and handed Ocky down onto the kitchen table below. The first thing he did was to move the kitchen table so that Ocky couldn't climb out again the way she'd come. Whilst Ocky explored he made quite sure that his den was escape-proof. He'd never before had to think of it as a place that no one should get out of, only as a place that no one should see into. The walls were sheer all around and although one wall was lower than the rest there were no footholds, no way of climbing out; and the tin trunk was pushed tight up against the hole in the wall. 'I've got you boxed in, Ocky,' he said.

The church bell rang five o'clock. Harry knew he'd better get home or else there'd be more trouble. Ocky was standing on the kitchen table trying to peel the paper off the wall above her head. She seemed totally absorbed in it. Harry left her quickly. He crept around the corner where she could not see him and set the ladder against the wall. Once at the top he hauled it up after him and hid it in the brambles. He went out the way he'd come in – over the wire.

He was brushing himself down on the front doorstep when there was a voice behind him.

'And where the devil have you been, Harry?' Bill's voice came out of the smog.

'I met a friend,' said Harry. 'I've been round in the park.'

'You've been told and told to come straight home on

nights like this. You know your mother'll be worried sick about you.' Harry knew she wouldn't be and sure enough she wasn't. Both Granny Wesley and Mother were bathing Georgie in the kitchen. They'd never even missed him.

'I've left your food in the oven,' said Granny Wesley, looking up at him as he came in. 'Just look at the state of him,' she said. 'What've you been up to now?' Fortunately they didn't really want to know. He ate his tea fast, worried already that Ocky might be upset at finding herself alone. 'Apples for afters,' said his mother.

He hadn't really thought about it till then. He'd have to find Ocky something to eat. Fruit, any kind of fruit, and vegetables, that's what Signor Blondini had said. His satchel was at his feet. He slipped the apple into it whilst no one was looking. But that would hardly be enough, he thought, not for the whole night. So as soon as they'd all gone upstairs to put Georgie to bed he made for the larder. Two onions and a cabbage, that was all he could find. That would have to do. He'd buy some tomorrow and replace them. With a bit of luck no one would notice, he thought, not unless they were using them for supper. He took them anyway and a couple of stale crusts out of the bread bin just in case Ocky liked bread.

Once down in the basement again Harry crept

towards the fireplace. He dragged aside the tin trunk as slowly as he could, but the sound of it terrified Ocky, sending her scampering and screeching into the corner of the den. 'Only me,' said Harry coming out of the hole head first and holding out the bread to her. 'It's only me. *Va bene . . . Va bene.*' Ocky huddled against the wall, her eyes blinking wildly. As he came closer she scratched her shoulder. She always seemed to do that, Harry noticed, when she was uncertain; and then she recognised him and came running towards him hauling herself up his leg and onto his shoulders. Harry sat her on the kitchen table and laid out the food in front of her. She took the bread at once and wolfed it down, every last crumb of it. Then she tackled the onions, both at the same time. The cabbage she seemed less keen on, but maybe, Harry thought, that's because she isn't hungry any more. They shared the apple offering it back and forth until all that was left was the core. She was very fastidious, picking out the pips before finishing it off.

'How do you like my den, Ocky?' Harry said. 'Not bad, is it? You've got a place to sleep over there, on the mattress. Come on.' And he took Ocky's hand and led her across to the darkest corner of the den and sat her down on the mattress. 'You've got a pillow, look, and there's blankets, too. Well, they're old curtains, really, but there's lots of them.' He threw Ocky curtain after curtain from the chest of drawers. Ocky rolled and romped amongst them, and then gambolled around the den trailing them behind her, Harry chasing her ineffectually and trying to retrieve them as they dropped off, but he was laughing so much that in the end he had to stop to catch his breath. He flopped down on the mattress and when Ocky realised no one was chasing her any more she joined him. 'I won't go to school tomorrow, Ocky,' he panted. 'I'll stay here with you if you like. I've done it before. It's easy when you know how. I wish I was a chimpanzee. No school, no Miss Hardcastle. You don't know how lucky you are.' Ocky lay on her back and played with her feet. 'I've got to go soon, Ocky. They'll begin to wonder else, but you got to promise me to make no noise otherwise they'll find you.' Ocky didn't seem to be listening. She was on her feet again, jumping up and down on the pillow and pounding it into the mattress. He took her hand and pulled her over to him. 'I mean it, Ocky, no noise, right? Promise me now.' He stroked her head behind her ears where he knew she liked it, and found himself being hugged tight round the neck, Ocky's fingers exploring the deepest recesses of his right ear. 'I'll be back tomorrow. I'll bring you some more food, too. Onions if

I can get them, but I'll need some money.' He climbed up to his money store high in the wall, took out his pencil box and emptied it. 'This should keep us going,' he said putting the pencil box back. 'Now you be good.'

He left her then sitting in the dark on the mattress. She made no attempt to follow him as he crawled back through into the basement. The last he saw of her, as he pushed the tin trunk up against the hole, she was rolling the cabbage around the den and chasing after it.

In the morning the smog was still there outside his window. Granny Wesley made lumpy porridge, and as usual she insisted he had to have salt in it and not sugar. Harry swallowed it quickly so that he didn't have to taste it. Granny Wesley pottered about the kitchen like she always did at breakfast, a cigarette hanging from her mouth, talking nineteen to the dozen. Harry wasn't really aware of what she was saying. She was background noise like the warm hum of the gas stove. 'Harry! Harry!' she was talking at him now. 'Are you listening to me, young man? I said did you hear the owl last night?'

'Owl?'

'I've never heard anything like it,' she said. 'Hooting and shrieking it was. Kept me awake half the night.'

Bill looked up. 'Couldn't have been an owl,' he said. 'We don't have owls here.'

'I'm telling you it was an owl. It came from the bombsite,' said Granny Wesley. 'I'm sure of it. I know an owl when I hear one.' And then it dawned on Harry what she was talking about.

'I never heard nothing,' he said.

'You never heard anything, you mean,' said Granny Wesley.

'Nor me,' said Bill pushing his chair back. 'You had a bad dream, Mother. We'd best get going, Harry. We'll be late.'

Harry knew Bill would walk him to the school gates – he always did these days, ever since he'd been caught playing truant. It would make it more difficult, of course, but he was quite determined that he would not go to school that day. As he closed the front door behind him, Harry saw that the smog was worse than ever, and that suited him well, very well indeed.

When Bill left him he actually went in through the school gates, waited in the corner of the playground until he was sure Bill was out of sight, and then walked out again. No one even noticed him – the smog was so dense. In the greengrocers' on the corner he bought all the onions and cabbages and potatoes his money could buy. The greengrocer – Martha she was called – always looked cold. Her hands and her cheeks were as purple as her beetroots. She was a bit surprised that he asked for quite so many onions. 'You sure, Harry?' she said.

'It's what Mum said,' he replied, shrugging his shoulders.

Then it was back to the bombsite, keeping to the other side of the road just in case he bumped into Granny Wesley going shopping. He found it just as difficult to climb the wire as he had done the day before – the links were too small for his feet. It was a slow climb. Just as he reached the top of the fence he heard footsteps coming along the pavement below. Harry froze where he was and held his breath as they passed beneath him. Whoever it was had only to look up to see him, but they didn't. Harry found the ladder and let himself down into the den. Ocky came scrambling across the den, hooting her welcome. He was climbed on at once and clasped passionately around the neck.

It was some moments before he could calm her down – and then he looked around him. The floor was a carpet of feathers, wall to wall. The table was upside down, the drawer hanging out. The stuffing in the armchairs had been ripped out. The chest of drawers was on its side and broken. Cigarette cards were scattered everywhere in amongst the feathers, and his conkers and marbles were strewn all over the place. The photograph of his father lay on the floor by the mattress, the glass broken; and the medal, his father's medal, was gone from the wall and was nowhere to be seen.

CHAPTER FIVE

'WHAT HAVE YOU DONE WITH IT, OCKY?' HARRY cried.

Nothing mattered to him now except the medal. He dumped Ocky unceremoniously into the armchair and began searching frantically on his hands and knees amongst the feathers. Ocky seemed puzzled at first, but then she began to whoop and screech and clap her hands. She leapt off the armchair and frolicked in amongst the feathers, throwing them up in clouds above her head and shrieking with delight at this new game.

But Harry had had enough. He shouted at her, 'Can't you see what you've done, Ocky, you stupid beast? You've gone and lost my dad's medal.' He took her by the shoulders and shook her. 'What've you done with it? Where've you put it?' Ocky screeched and scampered off into the corner where she huddled, whimpering and scratching herself. She looked back balefully at him over her shoulder.

Harry took pity on her and regretted his outburst at once. He thought he could make his peace with an onion and took one out of his satchel. He offered it to her slowly as Signor Blondini had told him and avoided looking at her directly in the eye. She moved away from him at first and then sat down sulking, and looked the other way. Harry put the onion gently on her lap and sat down beside her. 'I didn't mean it, Ocky,' he said. 'Honest I didn't. But it's my dad's, see. It's the only thing I got left of his.'

Ocky touched the onion and smelt her hand. 'I bought it for you special,' Harry said. He crawled over and picked up the photograph of his father and showed it to Ocky. 'Look Ocky, that's him, that's my dad. He got killed in the war. And you see there, that's his plane. That's a bomber that is, a Lancaster. He was in it when he got killed.'

Ocky picked up the onion and considered it.

'He was a hero, my dad was,' said Harry. 'He got himself killed just to save the others, Ocky. Honest he did. That's what he got the medal for. I told them at school and they don't believe me. They think I'm making it all up, but I'm not. He could've got out, Ocky, he could have. Mum told me all about it.' Ocky seemed to be listening now. Harry went on, 'They were coming back from France across the Channel and his plane got all shot up. The pilot was killed, and my dad – he was the navigator, my dad – he took the controls and tried to fly the plane back home across the Channel. But after a bit he knew they couldn't make it, so he told the others to jump out while they still could. Someone had to stay at the controls, see. He told them he'd jump later, but he never did. They all got picked up out of the sea. He saved their lives, Ocky. My dad should have got out too but he didn't – maybe he couldn't, I don't know. Anyway his plane crashed into the sea. That's why I've got to find his medal, Ocky.'

He put his arm round Ocky's shoulder and Ocky climbed onto his lap and bit enthusiastically into her onion. She looked up into Harry's face.

'I'm not crying,' said Harry, 'it's your onion making my eyes water, that's all.' He wiped the tears away with his wrist. 'How am I going to find it in all this mess? You're going to have to help me tidy up, Ocky. After all, it's your mess. You're a little monkey, aren't you?'

He laughed at himself then, and picked up some conkers under his leg. 'I don't mind about the cigarette

71

cards, not really, they'll dry out anyway; but it looks like you've had a good go at my conkers – there's teeth marks in them. I bet you tried every one of them didn't you?' He pushed Ocky gently off his lap and got to his feet. 'Still, we got all day to find the medal, haven't we? Got to be here somewhere, hasn't it?'

He left Ocky with her onion and began a systematic search. First he picked up all the feathers he could and stuffed them back into the pillow. Then he collected up the cigarette cards; some of them were torn and some were damp but, by the time he'd finished, all the sets were complete, except one. He thought Ocky must have eaten one or two. There was still no sign of the medal, so when he'd picked up all the marbles and conkers he led Ocky by the hand all around the den asking her where she'd hidden it, hoping she might find it for him intentionally or otherwise. He knew it was hopeless but it was all he could think of. She liked the walk but didn't seem to understand what it was for. In the end Harry gave up and concentrated on tidying the den, praying the medal might still turn up.

By the late afternoon the den was restored again, but the medal had not been found. Harry was sitting morosely in the armchair gazing up at a pigeon on the black support beams that propped up his house, when

Ocky sprang lightly up onto the kitchen table and reached up into Harry's money hole in the wall.

'It's all gone, Ocky,' he said. 'I spent it on your onions and potatoes, remember?'

When Ocky turned round again she had the pencil box in her hands. There was no lid on it. She reached in and took out the medal. Harry did not have to ask for it. Ocky brought it to him and offered it to him.

'Thanks Ocky,' he said, kissing the medal. He lifted her back on his lap and stroked her head. 'I can't make you out,' he said. 'I don't know what you understand and what you don't. It's like you knew all along what I was looking for, you rascal, you.' He sniffed at her. 'You stink of onions, you pick your nose, and you've wrecked my den. I've got nothing much to love you for, have I?'

Ocky studied the medal that Harry held out in front of her, touching it and smelling her fingers.

'What am I going to do with you, eh? I ought to take you back to Signor Blondini, I know I should. But they've got plenty of other animals in the circus, haven't they? And you're just as happy with me here, I know you are. And anyway what did you run away for in the first place, that's what I'd like to know? Maybe you weren't happy there. Maybe you don't want to go back at all. P'raps you came looking for me in the park. Is that what it was, Ocky? Signor Blondini told me you were always looking out for me. He said so, didn't he?' He looked down at her upturned face. 'So it's not stealing, not really. After all you came of your own free will, didn't you? It's not a sin, is it, not if I just look after you for a bit?' He chewed on the leaf of cabbage he was offered. 'Father Murphy knows all about sins. He'd tell me. That's what I'll do, I'll go and see Father Murphy and see what he says. If he says I've got to take you back then I'll take you back, I promise you I will, Ocky.'

Harry stuffed everything he could into his satchel, his marbles, his cigarette cards and the few conkers that were left unblemished by Ocky's teeth. He put the medal and his father's photograph into the pocket of his coat, threw the pillow full of feathers over his shoulder and began to climb the ladder up into the bombsite above.

Ocky was not happy to be left this time and she tried to climb up the ladder after him. Harry had a ready answer for this, though. He reached into his satchel and threw down a potato. She scampered after it leaving him enough time to climb to the top and pull the ladder up after him. When she saw what he'd done she came back, screeching furiously at him. 'Don't make so much noise, Ocky. Granny Wesley heard you last night, you know. Shhhh.' He put his finger to his lips and threw her another potato. Ocky ignored it but seemed more resigned now. She sat back on the floor of the den and scratched her shoulder. Harry stuffed the pillow behind a wall and climbed over into the road. He could just make out the church spire at the end of the street, a finger of dark in the smog.

It was the smell of the church that Harry liked best – that first smell when you walk in. As an altar boy he'd processed often enough up the aisle swinging the incense but he'd never really known what it was for. He'd thought maybe it was because Heaven smelt of incense; but how did anyone really know what Heaven smelt like, I mean no one had ever been there and come back had they?

Father Murphy was having his tea and biscuits in the vestry when Harry knocked on the door. 'I want to make my Confession, Father,' he said.

'It's the middle of my tea, Harry,' said Father Murphy, his mouth full of biscuit. 'Is it an urgent thing that can't wait?' Harry nodded. 'Come on then,' said Father Murphy. He bent down to switch off the single bar electric fire and they walked together down the aisle of the church towards the red glow of the sacristy light over the altar. 'And how's that little brother of yours?'

he said. 'I'll be baptizing him, next week you know.' Even Father Murphy has Georgie on the brain, Harry thought. 'You smell something awful,' said Father Murphy, his arm around Harry's shoulders.

'Onions,' said Harry patting his satchel. 'I'm taking some onions home for Mum.'

Once in the privacy of the confessional box, with the grille between them and Father Murphy shadowy on the other side of it, Harry began. 'Bless me, Father, for I have sinned.' There was a whole list of selected sins to be taken into consideration first, the worst being his recurring wish to kill Miss Hardcastle, before he got to the main one on his mind.

'Is that all you have to tell me, my son?' said Father Murphy. 'No little lies and hidden deceits you've left out?'

'Well there is something else, but I'm not sure if it's a sin or not, Father,' said Harry.

'Perhaps I'll be the judge of that,' said Father Murphy. 'It's what I'm here for.'

'Well, I think perhaps I've stolen someone, Father.'

'Stolen someone?' Father Murphy sounded alarmed.

'Well not exactly someone, not a real person, I mean.'

'Well what, then?'

'She's called Ocky. She's a chimpanzee,' said Harry. 'And she's my friend. I keep her at home, Father.'

He was careful not to mention the den.

'You keep a chimpanzee at home, my son?'

'Yes, Father. I met her in the park and brought her home with me. She wanted to come and now I don't want her to go. The thing is, Father, she belongs to someone else, really. Do I have to take her back? Is it a mortal sin to keep her?' He heard Father Murphy chuckling.

'No, my son. Not at all it isn't. I think maybe you're a bit lonely just now. Not many friends at school, is that it? Little Georgie has put your nose out of joint, has he? It's the most natural thing in the world in these circumstances for little children to invent a friend. I did it myself when I was a youngster. That's all you've done. You've got yourself a little friend. Now he may seem very real to you . . .'

'It's a she, Father, and I didn't make her up,' Harry protested.

'No, of course you didn't. That's the nature of things when you're lonely. You want a friend so badly that you make one up, but the trouble is you don't know you have, and that's why you think she's real. Just think about it and you'll know I'm right. You're feeling a bit lonely just now, aren't you, a bit unwanted?'

'I suppose so.'

77

'There you are then. Didn't I say as much? But when you're lonely, it's Jesus you should be turning to. You can trust him. He'll never let you down. What more could you ever want of a friend? Meanwhile an imaginary chimpanzee will do if it'll make you happy; and it's certainly no sin, so you've nothing to worry about. But when it comes to wanting to kill Miss Hardcastle that's a different matter. I've told you before. It doesn't matter what she does to you, it's a sin, a terrible sin, to wish her dead. An evil thought is a sin in itself, haven't I told you that before as well?'

'Yes Father.'

'Well then, you'll say three Hail Marys and you'll think no more wicked thoughts about Miss Hardcastle nor anyone else, do you hear me?' And that was that.

Harry came out of the church and made for home. He wondered as he walked along by the bombsite fence whether Father Murphy could possibly be right after all and that he had imagined the whole thing; but he only needed one look in his satchel at his soggy cigarette cards to know that Ocky was a live and living thing and that Father Murphy had got entirely the wrong end of the stick. I told him the truth, he thought, and it's not my fault he didn't believe me. And he did say it wasn't a sin, so I can keep Ocky as long as I like.

He ate his tea with relish, even though it was corned beef hash again. That pleased Granny Wesley greatly and she smiled at him and asked how it had been at school today. 'All right,' said Harry. She leaned forward and looked into his eyes.

'I don't think you've been to school at all,' she said. Harry was stunned. How could she have known? 'Close your mouth when you eat, young man,' she said, and she smiled again and reached out to touch his hair. 'I think you've been plucking chickens instead. Look at you!' And she held out a feather in front of his face. 'And there's two or three more in there.' And she laughed a shrill, witchy cackle. Harry's mother joined in.

'What's all the fun?' Bill said, closing the door behind him as he came in. Granny Wesley told him, and they all laughed again.

Throughout his bread-and-butter pudding there was the ceremony of Georgie's bathtime, with water splashing everywhere and laughter and Georgie screaming blue murder; and then they laid him down to power him, his legs kicking in the air. His mother was shaking powder on him and rubbing it in, and that gave Harry an idea.

'It keeps him from getting sore,' she said. 'You want to do it, Harry?' Harry shook his head. 'You can hold him afterwards if you like. You know you've never even held Georgie yet,' she said sadly. Harry could hardly bring himself even to look at Georgie let alone hold him.

'Now, there's something I'd like to know,' said Granny Wesley pointedly. 'Who took my onions? That's what I'd like to know.'

Harry closed his eyes fighting the surging panic inside him. He'd forgotten! He'd forgotten to put the onions back. He looked away so that they shouldn't see the blood rushing into his face. 'Shepherd's pie we were going to have tonight,' said Granny Wesley. 'I used up the last of the week's meat rations on some minced meat, and when I went to fetch the onions from the pantry they weren't there.'

'I'm sure they're in there,' said Mother. 'They were there yesterday and I certainly haven't used them. I saw them in the vegetable rack.'

Granny Wesley shook her head vigorously. 'You may think I'm old and a bit ga-ga, but when I say there are no onions I know it to be so. I looked myself in the vegetable rack and I'm telling you they're not there.'

Harry's mother gave in as she so often did and shrugged her shoulders. 'If you say so,' she said meekly.

Harry saw his moment and took it. 'I've seen them too,' he said. 'I'll fetch them if you like,' he said, and he went out hurriedly to his satchel that he'd left in the front hall. 'Here you are,' he said, coming back in. 'Two onions and a cabbage.' His mother beamed at him and that made his triumph all the sweeter. He dared not look at Granny Wesley's face.

He missed school the next day too. Bill saw him safely across the pedestrian crossing but as soon as Bill disappeared into the smog Harry crossed the road again and made for the bombsite. Ocky was waiting for him at the bottom of the ladder as he climbed down. Her welcome was ecstatic, so much so that she scratched his face with her nails. He'd brought the rest of the potatoes and the onions in his satchel today, and two of the potatoes seemed to keep her happy whilst Harry got ready for his performance.

A tin of baby powder would do the trick, he thought – and there was another tin left, so they wouldn't miss it – and his mother's old lipstick that he'd found thrown out in the wastepaper basket in the bathroom. Standing in front of the mirror he put the powder on, shaking it into his hands and patting his face till it was completely covered. It didn't seem to stick very well but the effect was just as he'd planned. He looked just like Mr Nobody. He was ghost-white now from the neck up.

There wasn't much left of his mother's lipstick but it was enough. He painted his lips a bright vermilion and then turned and faced Ocky who was still busy over her potatoes.

Ocky was delighted. She jumped up and down, she rolled, she somersaulted, she clapped.

When Harry pretended to play the violin, humming 'The White Cliffs of Dover', she hooted and screeched till Harry stopped for fear they might be overheard from the road. He tried to juggle with the potatoes. He couldn't but it didn't matter. Ocky seemed to understand what he was doing and she loved it all, picking up the potatoes whenever he dropped them – which was often – and handing them back.

He played clowns and circuses with her all that morning; and then it began to rain, driving them into the corner of the den under the ceiling where there was some shelter. Harry wiped off his make-up with a blanket and waited for the rain to stop. But Ocky soon tired of sitting and watching the rain. She ventured out to splash in the puddles, slapping at the water and jumping up and down in a frenzy of excitement. Then she settled down to drink, head down, in the biggest of them. Her thirst satisfied, she picked up one of the knives and began to scratch purposefully in the earth.

Harry watched her for some time and noticed how suddenly intent she had become. He called her several times but she would not come, so he went over to her. He discovered that she was scratching away at a small hole in the ground. Every now and then she was bending down to sniff in it. Harry squatted down beside her and cleared away the loose muddy soil. There was something metal sticking out of the ground, a dull rusty metal. He had no idea at all what it was at first, but then as he scraped at it with her, the shape became suddenly and horrifyingly clear.

He knew now what it was. It could be nothing else. He took Ocky's hand and pulled her back. He felt his heart pounding in his ears. He was looking down at the fin of a bomb. Of that there was no doubt at all, none whatsoever.

CHAPTER SIX

FOR JUST A MOMENT HARRY WAS PARALYSED
with fear. He'd trodden on that very spot hundreds of
times, and so had Ocky. He was overcome now by such
a confusion of alternatives that all he could do was stand
and stare. Then he stepped backwards slowly, holding
Ocky's hand in a firm grip. He skirted round the walls of
the den, his eyes never leaving the fin of the bomb. At
the foot of the ladder he wrapped Ocky round his neck
and climbed. He stumbled across the bombsite to the
fence and watched Ocky swing easily to the top. He
followed her hoping to goodness that Ocky would not
run off down the street. For a change Ocky was
obligingly co-operative and was waiting for him on the
pavement scooping her hand into the gutter and
drinking. Hand in hand they ran along the smog-filled

street, past the church and into the graveyard beyond.

The quickest way to the allotments was over the wall at the back of the graveyard. Father Murphy never liked people going that way but there was no time to lose. Before he could warn anyone about the bomb he had to find somewhere to hide Ocky and the only place he could think of was the allotments. There were maybe a dozen sheds on the allotments; Harry knew them all. He knew the allotments well because, along with the other choirboys, he had often helped Father Murphy with his vegetables. He chose the farthest shed away from the road, the corner one down by the railway line fence. It was the biggest shed, with a window looking out over the railway line, but no one used it any more now because it leaked and because it was leaning precariously downhill. Harry thought it wouldn't be locked, and it wasn't.

The door was tied shut with rotten string which gave way at the first tug. 'Here's your home for a bit, Ocky,' he said, 'until I can think of something better.' Ocky sprang up onto the workbench by the window and began pulling at the spiders' webs. She tried tasting them but evidently didn't care for them. Her nose wrinkled with disappointment or disgust and she jumped down to explore noisily amongst the garden pots and seed trays stacked in the corner. Harry was looking for a length of sound string to secure the door, but the best he could find was a roll of dusty twine. It was thin but there was enough of it to make it strong. It would have to do. He saw that Ocky had found a tray of seed potatoes and was busily sampling them.

It was the potatoes that reminded him that he'd left his satchel behind in the den. He would have to go back for it. If they found it there, then they'd know for sure he'd been using it, and his secret would be out. A few sticks of furniture, a few conkers, anyone could have left those there; but his satchel had his books in it, and his name on it. He didn't say goodbye to Ocky in case she protested, but just went. He tied the door quickly and ran back through the allotments. He vaulted the wall into the graveyard and dodged his way past the looming gravestones and crosses and statues; and then one of the statues seemed to move, reaching out and catching him by the arm.

'And what in Heaven's name are you doing, Harry Hawkins?' Father Murphy's voice stifled the scream in his throat. 'Aren't you supposed to be at school? What were you doing over there in the allotments? And haven't I told you not to use God's holy place as a thoroughfare?'

'It's a bomb, Father, it's a bomb,' Harry cried, trying to pull away from him.

Father Murphy held on to him fast. 'What's a bomb? What are you talking about, Harry?'

'I saw it, Father, honest I did.'

'I believe you, Harry, but you're not making any sense at all, and you won't, not until you calm down. We'll go into the vestry shall we, and you can tell me all about it.'

Harry had some time to work out what he would tell and what he would not tell, but always at the back of his mind was the thought of the incriminating satchel on the kitchen table down in his den.

'Now then, Harry,' said Father Murphy, taking off his cape and shaking it, 'you take a seat there and tell me what's on your mind.' Harry did as he was told.

'You won't tell anyone, Father?'

'You can talk to me in complete confidence, Harry,' said Father Murphy, 'you know that, but it's sounding more and more as if you've done something you ought not to have done.'

Harry could hardly deny that. He began his story. It was a garbled blend of half-truth and half-fiction, and he had the terrible feeling as he told it that Father Murphy knew exactly which was which.

'I saw it, Father, in the bombsite next to our house. It is a bomb, I know it is.'

'But where exactly did you find it, Harry? And mind you tell me the precise place now; it'll be most important.'

'It's in the middle of my den, Father.' He'd never intended to call it his den. It just slipped out inadvertently.

'Your den?'

'It's a sort of basement in the bombsite. I go there sometimes, that's all. It's a secret, Father.'

'But you're not allowed in the bombsite, Harry; no one is. It's a terrible dangerous place in there. You know that don't you? Anyway we won't bother with that little crime just at the moment. So you found the bomb and you were just coming to tell me, I suppose?' Harry nodded. 'Then you'll have to explain what you were doing coming from the opposite direction, from the allotments.'

'I was looking for you, Father. I thought you'd be in the church hall, and when you weren't there I took a short cut across the allotments to the church, that's all.'

'A short cut. I see. And so you'd like me to tell the police, I suppose; but at the same time you'd quite like it if I never mentioned that it was you that found it in the first place and you'd rather I never mentioned a word about your den? Is that about the gist of it, Harry?' Harry nodded. 'Are you being straight with me, Harry Hawkins, for if I've got to go out on a limb for someone I'd like to be sure that it doesn't break off, if you know what I mean.' Harry didn't, but he assured Father Murphy that it was all true about the bomb, every word of it. 'Very well then,' said Father Murphy standing up, 'we'd best be off and find ourselves a policeman then, hadn't we?'

They found one in the main street directing the traffic outside the school gates and helping the children back across the road from school.

'Constable,' called Father Murphy from the pavement, 'a quiet word in your ear if you please.'

'I'm a bit busy, sir, just at the moment,' said the policeman from the middle of the road.

'It's a matter of some urgency I assure you Constable,' said Father Murphy. The policeman waved the traffic on and came over.

'Well, sir?'

'It sounds unlikely, Constable, but I have to confess to a small crime.'

'You, sir?'

'Yes, me, Constable. You see, I was walking past the

bombsite down Philbeach Gardens, you know the place, do you?' The policeman nodded. 'And I heard this terrible yowling. I look down and I see this little kitten stuck behind the fence crying for its mother who's yowling her head off on my side of the fence. Well, you see my dilemma, don't you Constable? But anyway, stout as I am I climbed over, my intention being, of course, to reunite the mother and its infant. Now I know that that's trespassing and that I shouldn't have done it.' The policeman was beginning to show signs of impatience. 'That being said though, Constable, I thought in the interests of humanity it was a crime worth committing. Anyway the silly creature ran off the minute I approached it and so I followed it. I cornered it in a kind of bombed out basement place and after some difficulty managed to pick it up. I was just about to leave when I came across this bomb.'

'A bomb?' The policeman spoke too loudly and he knew it. 'A bomb sir? Are you quite sure sir?' he whispered.

'Oh yes Constable, I'm quite sure. I think I know a bomb when I see one.' Harry listened to all this in silent amazement and admiration.

Within a quarter of an hour the police were every-where, knocking at every door in the street emptying the houses. They were all being ushered along the road to the church hall when they heard the sirens and saw the army coming down the road in their lorries and Landrovers. As he looked over his shoulder Harry thought he could make out two of the soldiers moving around in the undergrowth beyond the fence and another was cutting a great hole in the wire. Father Murphy was walking beside him.

'Thank you, Father,' said Harry.

'As a matter of fact, Harry,' Father Murphy said and he put his arm around him, 'as a matter of fact I rather enjoyed it. Of course that's the trouble with sin, Harry. It is so damnably enjoyable. Anyway, it's only a little sin, and I'm sure we'll be forgiven an innocent little plot from time to time, specially if it saves lives. And I think your little secret's safe enough now.' But Harry knew that it wasn't. Sooner or later someone would find his satchel and there'd be questions he'd have to find answers for. They'd look inside and find not just school books but potatoes and onions. How on earth was he going to explain those away?

The entire population of the street was gathered in the church hall, and Harry soon found his mother, Georgie and Granny Wesley who was smoking frantically.

'Do you know it was right next door to us, Harry?' said Granny Wesley. 'We could have all been blown to bits in our sleep. It's all too dreadful to think about.'

Harry agreed. He saw Peter Barker coming his way, and walked away from his mother just in case Peter asked why he hadn't been at school for the past two days; and of course that's exactly what he did ask, and loudly too.

'Sore throat,' said Harry as hoarsely as he could manage. 'Temperature.'

'Better stay away from you then, hadn't I?' said Peter, smiling wryly. 'Don't want to catch it, do I?' And he went away laughing.

They were in the hall for less than a couple of hours before a policeman came in and announced that it was quite safe now for everyone to go home. The bomb was a dud, he said.

The talk at tea with Mother and Granny Wesley was all about the bomb. What would have happened if it hadn't been a dud? Were there any more in there? And who had found it, anyway? Wouldn't they just like to know, Harry thought, hiding the gristle from his shepherd's pie under his knife.

'Can I get down, please?' he said. There was still just the chance they hadn't found his satchel. He had to know, one way or the other. Granny Wesley pulled away his knife.

'All of it,' she said. 'You know my rules.'

'Eat up, dear,' said his mother. 'It'll do you good.' If Harry wanted to get to his den he knew he'd have to eat it otherwise he'd be sent to his room. He swallowed the gristle without argument and pushed away his plate.

'Can I get down now?' he said. And just then the door opened behind them.

'Not quite yet, Harry.' He turned round. It was Bill, and he had another man with him, someone Harry recognised instantly. It was the School Board man. He'd been round to the house twice before when Harry had played truant, but then it had been after a week or more – he'd only been away two days this time. 'Look who I met on the way back home,' Bill said putting his briefcase down on the dresser. 'I met him on the steps just outside the door, and he told me quite a story, didn't you, Mr Langley?'

'About the bomb, you mean,' said Mother.

'He told me about that too,' said Bill. 'It turned out to be a dud, I hear; just like someone else I know, not too far from here.' He put his hand on Harry's shoulder. 'I think you'd better stand up, Harry. Mr Langley wants to ask you a few questions and we'd all like to hear the answers.'

Mr Langley drew himself up to his full height, which was considerable, and thrust his thumbs in his waistcoat pockets. 'I told you I'd be round again, didn't I, Harry?' he said.

'He hasn't been missing school again, has he?' said his mother. 'He goes off every morning, good as gold. Bill takes him right to the school gates, don't you, dear?'

'It seems that's not enough,' said Bill. 'According to Mr Langley here he hasn't been in school for the last two days. Your son has been out in this smog wandering the streets. Anything could have happened to him.'

'Harry,' said his mother softly. 'Oh, Harry.' He could hear the pain in her voice.

'I told you the last time I was here, Harry,' said Mr Langley, 'I told you you had to go to school whether you liked it or not. I told you that, didn't I?' Harry nodded. 'Then why didn't you go?'

Harry blamed it all on Miss Hardcastle, and whilst this wasn't exactly true at least he didn't have to invent anything. He said he was too frightened to go to school and held out his still bruised hand as evidence. Bill took his hand and examined it, his brows furrowed. 'Miss Hardcastle did this?' he asked.

'With her ruler,' Harry said.

'Do you see this, Mr Langley?' said Bill.

'I do indeed, Mr Wesley. But it's no excuse, and I have my job to do. This boy must be in school. That's all there is to it. Now I'm warning you officially that it is your task, Mr Wesley, to make sure he attends. I shall not be warning you again. Is that understood?' He turned to go. 'And I've got my eye on you, my lad,' he said, wagging his finger at Harry. Bill showed him out through the front door.

Granny Wesley started as soon as he was gone. 'You see,' she said, 'he always finds someone else to blame it on. I tell you if I was Miss Hardcastle and I had that boy in my class I'd probably have done the same thing myself. After all, what else can you do with a boy like that, a boy that lies and lies like he does? I've often told Bill that he's been kind to him for too long. "Spare the rod and spoil the child." It's an old saying and a good one. If a child won't do what he's been asked to do then he must be made to do it. I've told him and I've told you.'

Harry's mother looked away and he saw there were tears in her eyes.

Bill had come back in again and shut the door behind him. 'That's enough Mother,' he said, and sat down heavily. 'Harry,' he said, 'there's things I'll say to you now I won't really mean. I'm at the end of my tether. I don't know what we're going to do about you, I really don't. So I'm going to have my tea and think about it. You'd best go to your room and do some thinking too. I'll be up later.'

Up in his room Harry sat on the edge of his bed and took the medal out of his trouser pocket. He breathed on it and polished the king's head on his pillowcase. He knew there was no escape now from the lecture that was to come and he was resigned to it. At least no one knew about his den, not yet anyway; and no one knew about Ocky either. As soon as the lecture was over he'd be able to creep down to his den and retrieve his satchel. If they had found it by now then they'd have brought it back. They must have missed it. He was sure of it now, or perhaps they'd seen it lying there and thought it was just part of the junk of the bombsite. Either way he was in the clear.

He lay back on his bed and thought of Ocky out in the cold of the allotment shed. She couldn't stay there for ever. As soon as all the hue and cry had died down he'd have to move her back into the den. Yes, that's what he'd do.

Then the doorbell rang. Harry heard voices downstairs.

'Mrs Hawkins, is it?'

'Mrs Wesley,' said Harry's mother. 'I *was* Mrs Hawkins.'

'Oh I see, madam, I see. You've got a boy, haven't you, Harry Hawkins?'

'Yes?' said Harry's mother.

'What's the matter?' It was Bill's voice.

'It's the police, Billy. They're asking about Harry.'

'He's been up to no good again, I know he has.' Granny Wesley was saying her piece.

Harry tiptoed to the door and opened it. He crawled along the passage and laid out flat on his stomach so that he could just peer through the banisters without being seen. He could see only the bottom half of the policeman, but that was enough. Harry's heart sank. He was holding his satchel in his hand. 'We found this. It's got his name on it.'

'Where?' said Bill.

'Well, that's the funny part. It's a bit of a mystery really. Do you mind if I come in, sir? It's a bit parky out here.' The door closed. 'Thank you. The truth is, sir, it wasn't us that found it. It was the army that found it, in the bombsite. Of course we've been in to have a look since.'

'The army?'

'Bomb disposal people. They brought it out with them after they'd taken the bomb away. They thought it looked as if it might belong to someone; and of course it does, doesn't it?'

'But I don't understand.' Harry's mother spoke in a hushed voice.

'Neither did we, madam. Neither did we, not at first. Here, take a look inside.' Harry could see the potatoes quite clearly from where he was. 'And there's an onion in there, too,' said the policeman, 'in amongst his school books. Funny, isn't it? So we took a look, like I said, after the army had left. It's quite a little set-up someone's got down there in the bombsite – chairs, tables, mirror on the wall, too. There is even a carpet on the floor. A proper little home it is, almost like someone was living down there.'

'Harry,' said Granny Wesley. 'It's Harry. It must be. I always wondered where he got to all the time.'

'You don't know it was Harry. How can you know it was Harry?' said his mother suddenly fierce. 'You're so quick to blame him. It could have been anyone. It could have been a tramp, couldn't it?'

'Of course, madam, like you say, it could have been anyone. But what was his satchel doing down there then, that's all I'd like to know? And we found a few other things down there we'd like you to take a look at. A couple of cigarette cards, for instance.' Harry could see them in his hand.

'They're his all right,' said Bill. 'He collects those.'

'There were lots of feathers scattered around, and a marble or two, and then we found these.' The policeman dug in his pocket and came up with a handful of conkers. 'Nothing strange about these, you may think, except that someone's had a bite out of every one of them. Someone, or something.'

'Something?' said Harry's mother. 'What do you mean "something"?'

'Well, madam, we can't be sure yet, but these conkers are baked, rock hard they are. Now you and me, we could hardly bite through a baked conker, could we? Some of these are bitten in half. Here, have a look for yourself. Now what we think, madam, is that your son was keeping some kind of a pet down there, and what's more we think we know what it was.' Harry's mother began to protest that it could have been a squirrel. 'It's not just the conkers, madam. We found bits of cabbage leaves, onion and potato skins. And, well, let's just say there was other evidence, madam, that there's been an animal down there.'

'You said you thought you knew what it was,' Bill said.

'A chimpanzee, sir. We think he's been keeping a chimpanzee down there.'

'But aren't they dangerous?' said Harry's mother.

'They can be when they're older,' said the policeman, 'but she's only a young one, and well trained. You see, she's from the circus. She went missing a couple of days ago. Perhaps she was stolen, perhaps she escaped, we don't know. All we know is that the owner of the circus, a Mr Blondini – Italian fellow I think he is – is very anxious to get her back. Now, we've looked everywhere, but there's been no trace of her, not until now, that is.'

'Goodness gracious me!' Harry could hear the gasp in Granny Wesley's voice. 'It was Harry all right. It must have been. You see, officer, I took him to the circus – it must've been a couple of weeks ago now, the night Georgie was born it was – and I remember that he took a special liking to the little chimpanzee, waving at it, he was, and calling him almost as if he knew him. I remember thinking it was strange at the time.' A long silence followed.

'No!' Harry's mother shouted. 'No! It's impossible. For a start, how did he get into the bombsite? That fence is far too high for him to climb. He couldn't have done it.'

'Well, you'd have thought so, madam,' said the policeman, 'but Father Murphy climbed it. It was him that found the bomb in the first place. He went in there to rescue a kitten, and we think your Harry was there with the chimpanzee, and they ran off when they heard Father Murphy coming. Besides, madam, we believe your boy had an easier way in and out of the bombsite. I don't know if you know it but there's a hole in the wall of your basement, a small hole I grant you, but quite large enough for a boy to climb through. There was a tin trunk pushed up against the hole on your side of the wall, like a sort of door really, and we think that's how he got in and out of the bombsite. You do have a basement room here, madam, don't you?'

'Yes,' said Bill, 'through that door, but we keep it locked all the time.'

'And the key?'

'In the broom cupboard,' said Bill.

'I think we'd better take a look, don't you, sir? Just to be sure, eh?'

Harry heard the key turn in the lock. He had already made up his mind to run. There was nothing else for it now. For one dreadful moment Granny Wesley stayed behind in the hall, blocking his escape route to the front door. Then muttering something about how she'd known all along that Harry was a bad penny, she followed them down the stairs. He inched down the stairs, treading near the wall where it was less creaky. He plucked his coat and scarf off the hook and opened the door slowly. He could hear them now dragging the trunk aside down in the basement and the sound of his mother crying. He closed the door as gently as he could and ran.

The street lamps were quite incapable of shedding any light in the thick gloom of the smog. He knew there were twenty-four of them between his house and the church – he'd counted them often enough – and he counted them now as he hared past each one. In the smog he might easily run past the church without even seeing it. He tried to miss the lady with her shopping basket but it was too late. He careered into her, knocking the basket out of her hands. He heard the curses and the tins rolling across the pavement as he fled.

He slowed to a walk in the churchyard and hugged the church wall. It was the long way round to the allotments but he didn't want to risk bumping into Father Murphy, not this time. An invisible train whistled and rattled as it steamed past below the allotments. Harry vaulted the graveyard wall and never once stopped running until he reached the shed.

'It's only me, Ocky,' he whispered through the door. '*Va bene. Va bene.*' And he wrestled with the string to get it undone. He wrenched at the last infuriating knot until it broke and the door opened. He went in slowly, talking all the while so as not to frighten Ocky. He expected an answering rustle from the corner, or a low hooting of welcome perhaps. None came. And then his feet crunched on broken glass. He looked across at the window beyond the workbench. It was broken. One pane was missing completely. He climbed up and leaned out of the window, but there was no sign of Ocky. The pane lay broken on the ground and the workbench under his hand was sticky. He smelt his fingers and knew that it was blood.

He cared no longer now about being caught. All that mattered now was to find Ocky. He ran from hut to hut through the allotments calling for her, stopping from time to time to listen. But he heard nothing except the shunting of trains and the rumble of traffic beyond. In the graveyard he leaned back against the church wall to catch his breath and collect his thoughts. What would she do? Where would she run to from here? It could only be the bombsite. It was the only place that she knew and she knew the way there. She'd be there. She had to be there.

He was running down the path away from the church door when he heard a soft hooting behind him. He turned. The church door was open and Ocky was standing there, one hand on the latch. He ran towards her and knew at once he shouldn't have done it. She screeched and scampered back into the church. Harry followed her in. She hadn't gone far. She was sitting in the font just inside the church door.

'Come on, Ocky,' he said softly. *Va bene. Va bene.* It's me, Ocky. Don't be frightened. It's Harry.' Ocky scratched herself on the shoulder and considered him for some moments before reaching up and grasping the beam above her head. Harry watched helpless as she swung herself easily up from one crossbeam to another until she was hanging by a foot and a hand from the handrail of the gallery above. She looked down at him, hooting; and the echo of it filled the church. 'Ocky,' Harry whispered. 'You've got to listen to me, you've got to understand. They're after us and we've got to get away. Come on, Ocky, come on down, please. Please. *Va bene, va bene.*' Ocky ignored him and swung herself up onto the rail. She walked along it and then jumped down onto the front row of seats on the other side. For some moments she vanished completely and then reappeared at the far end of the row where she stood up and clapped her hands, evidently delighted with her acrobatic skills.

Harry made his way to the belfry door that led up first to the gallery and then into the belfry above. He climbed the narrow winding steps slowly and when he emerged from the door into the gallery, Ocky was waiting for him on all fours, whooping her welcome. She climbed up his arm and hooked her arm around his shoulder. She kept licking the palm of her right hand and whimpering at him. 'Cut your hand on that glass, didn't you?' Harry said, catching her hand to try to examine it. He couldn't see too well, but he could feel it was still bleeding. 'We've got to wash it, Ocky; but first we've got to get out of here.'

They were half way back down the stairs when Harry heard voices. He recognised two of them at once, Miss Jefford, the organist, and Father Murphy; but there were more, many more. The lights in the choir came on and he heard the sigh as the organ started up. There was a babble of excited voices from the choir stalls now at the far end of the church and Father Murphy's voice was booming out: 'That'll be quite enough of that, boys. You're jabbering like a lot of monkeys. Yes, I know all about the little excitement. The bomb was there and now it's not there and that's as much as there is to say about it. Now if we're all here we can make a start.'

Of course. It was Friday evening and choir practice. Ocky had only to utter one of her hoots or shrieks and it would all be over. Once they were singing Harry thought they could make it to the door of the church just so long as they kept low behind the pews. He knew from experience that from up in the choir stalls you could see very little in the blackness of the back of the church. He'd bide his time until they got started. He sat down on the bottom step of the staircase and held Ocky as tightly as he dared.

'Is everyone here now?' Father Murphy asked.

'Harry's not,' said Peter Barker, 'but then he's got a sore throat. That's what he told me, anyway.' There was a chorus of sniggers quickly silenced by Father Murphy.

'Is that so? Well then, we'll have to start without him, won't we? We'll begin with "Hail Glorious Saint Patrick" just to limber up and loosen the throats.'

'*Va bene, va bene*, Ocky,' Harry whispered, praying hard that the magic in those words was still potent. 'Not a sound now, please.'

They sang the first two lines of the hymn before Harry made his move. He had his head out of the doorway and was crouching down ready to run when he saw Bill striding in through the church door. Harry froze where he was. Bill walked up the aisle and tapped Father Murphy on the shoulder. Father Murphy stopped conducting and hushed the choir, but the organ played on for a moment or two before it fell silent. The two men were talking animatedly and walking back now towards Harry and Ocky. The choir behind them was chattering so loudly that Harry could only catch snatches of their conversation, but he could hear more and more of it as they came closer.

'He just ran off, Father,' Bill was saying. 'We've no idea where he could be, no idea at all. The police are out looking for him now; but in this smog we're not likely to find him, not unless we know where to look. I just came on the offchance that perhaps you'd seen him.' Father Murphy said nothing. 'He likes you, Father. We know he does. He talks to you.' They were no more than a few feet away from Harry now. 'He doesn't say much to me, Father, and that's my fault, I know; but he doesn't say much to anyone these days, not even his mother. I thought maybe he might have said something to you, though.'

'About what exactly?' said Father Murphy.

'Well you're not going to believe this but it seems

probable that he's been looking after a chimpanzee. He's been keeping it as a pet down in the bombsite by our house, where you found the bomb yesterday.'

Father Murphy reached out and put his hand on Bill's shoulder.

'Jesus Mary Mother of God,' he whispered. 'Did you say a chimpanzee?' Bill nodded. 'What have I done?' said Father Murphy. 'What have I done?' He turned to the choir. 'That'll be all for tonight, boys. We'll have to do it on Sunday without a practice. We've done it before. Quick! Quick! Off you go now. I've got things to attend to. Miss Jefford, you'll lock up for me, will you?' He turned to Bill. 'Mr Wesley, I can't explain it to you, but let's just say I've been a little unwise, no, I think stupid may be a better word for it. I think I must begin to make amends. I have a small inkling where your son might be hiding. The allotments. There's places enough there to hide a dozen chimpanzees. I saw him coming out of there this afternoon, going like a bat out of hell he was, if you'll pardon the expression. Come along now. I'll show you.'

The choir had gone and Miss Jefford had left the church to its hollow silence. Harry emerged from the doorway holding Ocky's hand.

'He's a Judas,' said Harry, the tears flooding down his face. 'He's a Judas like all the rest. It's you and me now, Ocky. Just you and me.'

CHAPTER SEVEN

ONLY THE FLICKERING GLOW OF THE SACRISTY lightened the darkness around them as Harry felt his way to the church door. There was just a chance that Miss Jefford had forgotten to lock it properly. After all, she was a dithering old soul, always playing a verse of a hymn too many or too few; but the door was indeed firmly locked. Harry wasn't that worried, though. There was still the vestry window. It was a bit small and he knew there was a long drop to the ground outside but he could jump it if he had to, he was sure of it. Clutching Ocky's hand he made his way to the vestry. He took the key out of the lock and once inside locked the door behind them. He felt safer that way. He had to climb up on the shelves to reach the window.

As soon as he opened it he heard the voices. They

were some way off still, but coming towards him. Torchlights, dim in the smog, danced in the darkness. At first he thought the squeaking must have been twigs rubbing up against a nearby window but then he heard the panting and saw the dogs straining on their leashes, noses to the ground. He closed the window and ducked down shutting out the noise. He gathered Ocky into his arms, hands over her ears so that she wouldn't hear the dogs, and they held each other in the dark as the footsteps passed by below the window.

'Nothing here, Sarge. The dogs aren't picking anything up,' someone said.

'Every inch of the churchyard, the Inspector said,' came another voice, 'and that's what we'll do. We've got to be a hundred and ten per cent sure they're not here.'

And then they were gone. Harry put Ocky down on the ground and let her go. He dared not risk lighting a candle even with the curtain drawn. Just one little chink of light could give them away. 'We'll have to wait in here for a bit, Ocky,' he whispered. 'There's dozens of them out there, and they've got dogs. All we've got to do is to keep quiet and sooner or later they'll go looking somewhere else.' His eyes were seeing better now through the blackness.

Ocky had Father Murphy's cupboard open and was

sampling the candles. She tried smelling them; then she chewed them, and finally she used them as drumsticks on the cupboard door until Harry took them from her; but he knew he'd have to find some way of keeping her both happy and quiet. Food was the only sure way to do that. Father Murphy always kept a supply of his digestive biscuits in the big dried milk tin on the mantelpiece, and Harry soon had Ocky settled on a chair and was plying her with biscuits. Fortunately there were plenty of them. So long as she had two at a time she seemed happy to sit there and would even offer Harry a bit from time to time. When she did get restless he would talk to her, sprinkling everything he said with lots of *'va bene'*s.

'What're we going to do, Ocky?' he said. 'Even if we do get out of here, where are we going to go? We haven't any food, I haven't got any money even. We can't go home, that's for sure. Anyway, I'm never going home again, Ocky. Never. Mum won't miss me much, not now she's got Georgie. She wasn't always like that, Ocky. It's Bill that's done it. Ever since she met him she's been different. She thinks he's wonderful – can't think why. He's always telling me what to do and what not to do. None of his business, is it? I'm not his son. I'm nothing to do with him, am I? Do you know what he was in the war, Ocky? He was a conchy – didn't want to fight; and you know why, Ocky? Because he's a coward, that's why. Do you know what he did in the war? Do you? He drove an ambulance, that's what he did. You don't win wars just driving ambulances, and you don't win any medals either, do you Ocky?'

He took his father's medal out of his pocket. 'Distinguished Flying Cross this is. My dad's medal.' Ocky reached out for it, but Harry held it out of her reach. 'He tried to take it away from me once, Ocky. He said it was precious to my mum and that I'd lose it if I carried it around everywhere, but it wasn't that. He was jealous, that's all. He hid it away in his desk, but I found it and put it in my den where he'd never find it. And he wouldn't have my dad's photo in the sitting room. I heard him and Mum arguing about it. I heard them. He said it wasn't good for me to grow up with the ghost of my father in the room. He just wants me to forget him so *he* can be my father instead. I'll never forget my dad, no matter what Bill does. I hate him, Ocky. Father Murphy says I shouldn't but I do. Anyway, what do I care what Father Murphy says any more? He's on their side, isn't he? Not like you. You're on my side, aren't you, Ocky?'

Ocky offered him a crumb of her biscuit and he took

it. 'That's all I get, is it?' he said, holding out his hand for more. 'I like digestive biscuits. Aunty Ivy gave me digestive biscuits when we were in Bournemouth. That's where Mum and me went on holiday and that's where she met Bill – on the pier at Bournemouth, it was. But Aunty Ivy, she's nice, Ocky. She liked me. She said if she'd ever had a son she'd have wanted him to be just like me.'

The window shook in its frame as a train thundered by at full steam, so fast that Harry could hardly distinguish the beat of the wheels on the rails before it was gone. He listened until the sound of it died in the distance. 'I've been on a train just like that,' he said, 'when I went to Bournemouth. Doesn't take long to get there.'

Until that moment he had never even thought of it, but he grasped now at the idea as a drowning man might a lifebuoy. 'That's it, Ocky!' he said, a little too loudly. 'That's it! Aunty Ivy! We'll go and see Aunty Ivy. She'll look after us, I know she will. She always said she'd help me if I ever needed her. She said so. It's the same railway line, Ocky; it goes right by the church, I know it does. I've stood and watched them on the bridge dozens of times. When the signal's up they go roaring through like that one, and then when the signal's down they stop just before the bridge. All we've got to do, Ocky, is to be there when one of them stops, and an hour or two later we'll be in Bournemouth. Easy as pie. We could do it, Ocky, we could! And you'll like Aunty Ivy. We can stay with her as long as we like. She said so on her Christmas card. She invited me, Ocky.' Ocky stiffened suddenly and whimpered. Harry heard it too, now. *'Va bene,'* he whispered to her. *'Va bene.'*

The church door yawned open, the light from the choir flooding in under the vestry door. Father Murphy was talking.

'I'm telling you they couldn't possibly be in here. Miss Jefford locked the place after choir practice and he certainly wasn't in here then.'

'We'd just like to make quite sure, Father,' said another voice. 'We'll take a little look around, if you don't mind.'

'Help yourself,' said Father Murphy, 'but you'll not find anything.'

Harry listened at the door as the footsteps went away down the aisle and then came back towards them.

'What's in there?' The voice was close now, just on the other side of the door.

'The vestry.' Father Murphy sounded irritated. The handle turned and the door rattled. 'Locked?' said

Father Murphy. 'It's not usually locked. Here, let's have a try,' and the handle turned again. Harry pulled Ocky closer to him and stroked her on the head behind the ears. She was taut in his arms and listening hard.

'That's Miss Jefford for you, officer,' said Father Murphy with a chuckle. 'Tell her to lock up and she'll either forget altogether or she'll lock every door in sight. She locked me in there once, I remember, while I was having my tea.'

'I ought to take a look inside, Father. We've been told to look everywhere.'

'You're welcome to. I've got a key back in the house, but it's not likely they'll be in there, is it? I mean if it's locked for us it'll be locked for them, won't it? It seems to me to be asking a bit much, don't you think, for them to have gone through one locked door – but through two, they'd need a miracle. Now I'm a great believer in miracles, officer, but that would strain even my credibility. If you ask me,' said Father Murphy, walking away now, 'Harry Hawkins will be long gone by now. If you were him, would you hang around here with all that kerfuffle?'

'I suppose I wouldn't, Father.'

'Well then, there you are,' said Father Murphy. 'After you, officer.' And Harry heard the church door shut behind him and could breathe again.

As the time passed, despite all his efforts to contain her, Ocky lapsed more and more into a talkative hooting quite loud enough to be heard outside the church, Harry thought. But there was nothing at all he could do about it. Every few minutes now he would climb up onto the shelf to listen at the window but all sounds of men and dogs had long since gone. He had to be quite sure, though, so he determined to wait until ten o'clock struck on the church clock before he made a move. He could tell by now which trains were going to stop at the signal by the bridge. He could hear the hissing and clattering from far away and then the squealing of iron on iron as they ground to a halt just outside the church. He had worked out that if the signal stayed down for long enough there could be just enough time to get out of the vestry window, run across to the railway line fence and climb over.

When ten o'clock struck at last he was ready. 'You've got to stick close to me, Ocky,' he said, 'and for God's sake don't go running off; you'll ruin everything. *Va bene. Va bene.*'

With Ocky on the shelf beside him, Harry opened the window and waited for the clunk of the signal as it fell and the sound of the next slow train in the distance.

One fast train roared by, and then he heard the signal go down, and from some way off still the sound of a slowing train. 'I'll go first, Ocky,' he said. He put one leg out of the window and pulled the rest of himself through. It was a tight squeeze. He waited for Ocky to join him on the ledge outside and then he took her hand and jumped. It was a lot further down than he'd thought, and he fell awkwardly as he hit the ground. Ocky rolled over and was on her feet and scampering about, rejoicing in her new-found freedom. Harry lay where he'd fallen trying to stifle the cry of pain that welled inside him. He was clutching at his ankle and groaning in agony.

Ocky thought he was playing at first and began to wrestle with him until Harry found the strength to push her off and pull himself to his feet. Ocky seemed upset at his rejection and sat sulking and scratching herself under the trees. She wouldn't even look at him. '*Va bene, va bene,*' said Harry, beckoning Ocky back towards him. Ocky would not take his hand but she followed Harry through the trees and down towards the railway fence. She didn't have to be asked to climb it, she was hanging from the top before Harry had even begun to climb. He could see the white smoke of the train as it came puffing through the smog towards them, the wheels grinding to a halt. Harry could climb with only one foot, hauling himself up by his hands. To put any weight on his other foot was impossible. It was a slow climb up over the fence and just as slow down the other side. But at last he found himself on the ground with the train panting in the darkness in front of him.

Far from being frightened of the hiss and sigh of the engine Ocky seemed positively excited by it, hooting and shrieking as she scurried down the embankment towards the train. Harry limped after her calling for her to come back. It was a goods train as Harry hoped it would be at this time of night. Ocky had picked up a stick and was banging the ground and screeching. At least no one will hear her, thought Harry, not with all the noise of the engine. He had worried they might be spotted down on the railway track but both the engine at one end and the guard's van at the other were hidden in the smog. No one would see them. 'Come here, Ocky, come back here. *Va bene, va bene.*' And to his great surprise and relief Ocky came scuttling back to him, waving her stick in the air.

Harry had never realised until he was down by the railway track just how high the wagons would be off the ground. There was no conceivable way he could climb up. There were no handholds and no footholds.

He heard the signal go up, and then Ocky suddenly broke free of his grasp and ran along the track beside the train. Before he had time even to call her she had swung herself up onto the buffers in between two of the wagons. Harry followed as best he could. He had just managed to haul himself up and was standing on the buffers when he heard the first chuff of steam. He braced himself and clung to the cross girders at the back of the wagon as the train jolted forward. He looked up. Ocky was gone but he could hear her now screeching inside the wagon. He managed to get one good foothold where the girders crossed and heaved and pulled himself upwards, reaching for the top of the wagon. He hung there for a minute or two as the train gathered speed and steamed under the bridge engulfing him in smoke. His arms were shaking now, both with fear and with the strain of it. With his good foot as a lever he swung his other knee up and over the top, and gripped with the crook of it. He felt safer now and hung there for some time, summoning up the final effort he would need to drag himself up and over into the wagon and safety. The last part proved the easiest, though, and he let himself down as gently as he could, hanging from both hands. He landed on his one good foot and rolled over. Ocky was on top of him at once and they lay hugging each other in the bottom of the empty wagon as the train steamed away into the night.

Ocky, it seemed, managed to find joy even in the most unlikely places. Whilst Harry cowered from the wind in the corner of the wagon, knees drawn up to his chin to keep out the cold, Ocky explored and experimented. Everything that had found its way into the wagon, a torn tarpaulin, an old newspaper, sweet papers, twigs and leaves, all were investigated keenly, smelt, tasted, torn apart or simply studied. Anything and everything was of interest to her but clearly best of all was the large metal nut that rattled and banged as she threw it around the wagon and chased after it hooting wildly. She seemed fascinated by the hollow echoes of the wagon and kept hooting and listening, waiting for the sound to bounce back at her and each time it did it caused more excitement and more hooting. Harry wondered if there would ever be an end to it, but the entertainment she provided took his mind off his ankle, temporarily at least.

It throbbed mercilessly. He felt it from time to time and each time it seemed bigger. He tried to wriggle his toes inside his shoes. If you could do that then it wasn't broken – that's what he'd been told. He found he could wriggle some of them, but not all of them, and he wasn't sure what that meant. But broken or not it was difficult to forget about it even with Ocky's distracting antics.

The open iron cell of the wagon offered little protection from the wind and none whatsoever from the cold night air. He pulled the tarpaulin up around him but it was damp and seemed to make little difference. The only warmth to be had was from Ocky. When she had exhausted all the delights of the wagon and at last become bored with the nut and the sound of her own hooting, she came over and clambered in with him under the tarpaulin.

'You can see the sea from my room at Aunty Ivy's, Ocky,' he said. 'I don't suppose you've ever seen the sea, have you? It looks as if it goes on for ever and ever like the sky. You'll see. I'll take you to the beach, Ocky. She's got a swing in her garden, too. Bet you've never been on a swing either, have you? And you just wait till you taste her toad-in-the-hole, and her bread-and-butter pudding and her bubble-and-squeak. And in the evenings you have cocoa and digestive biscuits. Aunty Ivy, she always has digestive biscuits. You like them don't you, Ocky?' But Ocky was asleep. Harry looked up and saw that there were stars above him now instead of smog. A few minutes later a smoky moon was riding the sky above him filling the wagon with light. Harry was wondering as he dropped into sleep whether the moon would stop if the train did.

They were both woken at the same time. The regular rocking that had lulled them to sleep was losing its rhythm. The train jolted and jarred until it came at last to a juddering standstill. Ocky stood up beside him scratching her shoulder and lifting her head to listen. In the distance the engine breathed slowly, and then there were voices coming along the track. Ocky whimpered and before Harry could stop her she was walking across the wagon on all fours hooting softly. Harry went after her but tripped over the torn edge of the tarpaulin and fell heavily and noisily. Ocky came over and sat on his leg looking at him as he lay there. The footsteps were crunching on the stones just outside their wagon.

'Did you hear something?' said a voice.

'You're always hearing things, Benjy.'

'No, honest; like a sort of owl it was.'

'Well maybe it *was* an owl,' said the first voice. 'Come on, let's get on with it.'

'Owls don't bump around, do they? I heard something bumping in that wagon. Honest I did. One of these wagons here. I've never liked this place. Gives me the shivers.'

'Look Benjy, I want to get home tonight. If you want

to go looking for bumps in the night on your own time that's your business, but we've got to get these wagons uncoupled and then we've got to get back to the depot. Now stop messing about and give us a hand here will you?'

There was much banging and clanking and not a little cursing before they went away, still arguing. Harry felt safe enough now and let go of Ocky's hand. The engine got up steam, and the wagons shuddered for a moment and were still again. There could be no doubt about it. They were being left behind. Harry's plans were ruined. They'd never get to Bournemouth, not now. The engine chugged into the night leaving them to the moonlight and the silence.

Ocky seemed strangely unsettled and began to run around the wagon, stopping every so often to stand up and listen. Then she would sit for a few moments, elbows on her knees, and scratch herself on her shoulder before setting off once again around the wagon. Harry talked to her to try to calm her. Something was upsetting her – that much was quite clear. Talking did not seem to help, no matter what he said. Even *'Va bene, va bene,'* Signor Blondini's magic words, seemed to have lost their effect. He went over to her slowly and tried to put his arm around her. It was then that her whole demeanour suddenly changed. She glared at him, her lips pursed, her eyes full of anger. He backed away, averting his eyes from hers as Signor Blindini had once told him and talking all the while to try to reassure her.

'What's the matter with you, Ocky? *Va bene, va bene.*' Ocky began to sway slowly from side to side, and then with no warning at all she charged at him, screeching with fury and stamping as she came. Harry was backed up against the wall of the wagon. There was nowhere to run to. He held up his arm to protect himself and closed his eyes. Ocky sprang at him, one hand grasping his coat and another his shoulder. He felt the weight of her as she climbed up him, put one last foot on his head, and sprang up reaching for the top of the wagon to swing herself over. It had all happened so fast that there was no time for fear, only for disbelief at Ocky's transformation into a wild animal.

Harry heard her land on the stones outside and then there was silence. Strangely he did not feel in any sense rejected. He sensed no personal animosity. Ocky had wanted to escape and that was all. The wagon had become a cage to her, Harry thought, and she had to get out. But why here, and why so suddenly? That was what he could not understand. He was trying to work it all out when it occurred to him that the wagon was a cage to him as well and that he too was trapped inside it. The sides all round were high and smooth – even Ocky had needed him as a springboard to get out. He stood on tiptoe and reached up. His fingers were still some way from the top. If he sprang up and down on his good foot he could just about reach the top but only to touch it, not to grip it. He would have to take a run at it using the entire length of the wagon. But with his left foot hindering him he could not get up enough speed, so that he managed only to grasp the top with his fingers but did not have the impetus to pull himself up. And to make matters worse his hands were so numb now with the cold that he could scarcely grip with them anyway. He began to despair, hurling himself again and again uselessly at the side of the wagon, frantic to get out and find Ocky. At last, exhausted and dejected, he sank down on the tarpaulin in the corner. He could not do it. Terrible thoughts of dying there alone in the wagon from starvation or cold ran through his mind. He turned over on his stomach and pummelled the tarpaulin in this frustration.

It was the feel of the damp tarpaulin against his cheek that gave him the idea. He dragged the tarpaulin across the floor of the wagon and folded it as thickly as he could to make a kind of a step out of it, and then he backed into the far corner and charged, shutting out the pain in his ankle. The step provided the few extra inches he needed. He had the purchase now to haul himself up so that one arm was over the top. He kicked out frantically, scrabbling at the side of the wagon, and managed at last to hook one knee over. He rested there for a few moments to get his breath back and to see if there was any sign of Ocky. He called out, his voice ringing in the wagon below him. 'Ocky! Ocky! *Va bene, va . . .*' And he stopped short. He had only just realised what it was that was shimmering out there in the moonlight. It was a field of tanks. They filled the meadow from the railway line right across to the line of dark trees in the distance. They were lined up there in ranks, some with their turrets open, others their guns pointing towards the stars. He called again and a dog began to bark back at him from somewhere far away. Harry let himself down carefully on to the buffers first, and from there down onto the railway track.

He scrambled under a barbed-wire fence, and then he was walking in amongst the glistening tanks and calling again for Ocky. He reached out to touch the barrel of a gun and the white of the frost came off on his fingers. He called once more and the same distant dog replied. There were no tracks to follow so he had no idea at all where Ocky could have gone. As he wandered through the tanks he came upon some sheep grazing in the moonlight. They scattered silently when they saw him, like white ghosts, he thought, flitting through a graveyard of tanks.

Harry had stopped to stare back at a tank with a gaping hole like an eye in front of it, its gun barrel pointing directly at him. It was then that he heard the music. At first he thought that he must be dreaming but then it came again, louder this time and more distinct, more tuneful. He recognised the instrument at once. It was a violin.

CHAPTER EIGHT

HARRY STOOD AND LISTENED, LEANING UP AGAINST the tracks of a tank to take the weight off his ankle. It was some kind of dance tune, the rhythm spritely and constant, and then it stopped. He could hear laughing voices, one man's voice louder and more raucous than the others. So absorbed had he become in the music that Harry had almost forgotten about Ocky; but then he heard her hooting, and at that moment he began to understand all her fury back in the wagon. The violin started playing again. There was no other explanation he could think of. Ocky must have heard the violin before he had – he'd often noticed how acute her hearing was. And to her the sound of a violin could mean only one thing – Mr Nobody. She'd run off to find Mr Nobody.

Harry limped from tank to tank towards the music and the laughter until he saw one of the tanks ahead of him flickering with the orange light of a fire. He moved more carefully now, keeping to the dark side of each tank. The voices were clearer. He could hear the cry of a baby starting up and a woman's voice comforting it. He could see shadowy figures around the fire. He could smell the smoke of it. There was only one tank now between him and the fire. He went down on all fours and crawled forward through the cold grass until he was as close as he could safely get. He lifted his head and felt the warmth of the fire on his face. Ocky was crouching beside the fire waving a stick in her hand. He counted one, two, three people around the fire. One of them had a baby over her shoulder and one was playing the violin. The last was sitting hunched by the fire.

'Well, and what have we here?' The voice came from above him. Harry looked up. The man glowered angrily at him, his face flickering bronze in the light of the fire. He wore a cap on the side of his head. He called out, louder this time and more harshly, 'Lookee here what I've found!' The violin stopped playing. He was holding two dead rabbits by the feet, their noses only a few inches from Harry's eyes, their ears flopping against his face. He pushed them away in disgust. 'We got a visitor,' the man said, grasping Harry by the arm and pulling him to his feet. 'Looks like we got a village lad here. Come to spy on the tinkers, have you?' Harry was dragged into the light of the fire. 'Well, you wanted to have a look, now you've got a look.' Ocky had seen him and began to hoot her welcome. 'What the devil's that?' said the man, the grip on Harry's arm loosening. Ocky was running towards him now and the man with the rabbits let go of him and backed away.

'It's a little g'rilla, Rollo,' said a slurred voice from the other side of the fire. It was the man with the violin. 'We've got a pair of them, by the looks of it – a boy and a little g'rilla.' Ocky was clambering up onto Harry's shoulder now, the stick still in her hand. 'Looks to me like they came together,' the violin player went on. 'Know each other, do you? If you've come prying like Rollo said, I'll teach you. I'll teach you.' And he lurched towards Harry. Ocky shrieked at him and waved her stick so violently that she dropped it.

'Leave him be, Zak,' said the woman holding the baby. 'Haven't you done enough for one night? You come back stinking drunk again and wake us all up.'

'All right, so I've had a few,' said the man with the violin. 'Where's the harm in that, eh? I play better when I've had a drink or two, you know I do. 'Sides, you saw it. That g'rilla likes it, doesn't he? You saw him clapping his hands, didn't you? I tell you, I thought I was dreaming, Rollo. Playing away I was all on me own and suddenly he's there, that little g'rilla, sitting right beside me. Couldn't believe me eyes. Thought it was the drink at first. Anyway, he starts clapping and hooting and I keeps playing and he keeps hooting. Never seen a g'rilla before.'

'She's a chimpanzee,' said Harry, and they stared at him. No one spoke for some moments.

'Hurt your foot, have you?' Harry wasn't quite sure who had spoken until the hunched figure by the fire beckoned him over. He was sitting on a log, a blanket wrapped around him, and as Harry walked over towards him he saw there was someone else with him under the blanket. The eyes of a young girl gazed up at him.

'You pick a funny time to call,' he said and Harry could see now that he was an old man. His hair was yellow-white and hung down to his shoulders. He had a pipe in his hand. 'Sit down and I'll take a look at your foot.' Harry sat down beside him on the log, shivering as he soaked in the warmth of the fire. 'Don't just stand there staring, Rollo,' said the old man sharply. 'Go and fetch the boy a blanket before he dies of the cold.' The young man who had found him ran off into the darkness. 'Get your shoe off, boy, and put your foot up on my knee. I'm too old to bend down.' The girl's eyes never left Harry's face. He could feel them on him but could not bring himself to look back at her. The old man's hands were warm on his leg as he peeled the sock off. He wrapped his hands around it. 'Twisted it, did you?' Harry nodded.

Ocky climbed down off him and went to squat in front of the fire. She seemed completely entranced by the licking flames and hooted at them softly. 'Witchhazel, Meg,' said the old man. 'You know where it is. Be quick about it.' And the girl was gone at once, running away from the fire and up the steps into a caravan. She ran, Harry thought, like a cat runs, with no effort whatsoever. He could see two horses browsing beside the caravan in the half darkness. 'My grand-daughter, she is,' said the old man pointing with his pipe. 'And that's my grandson there. Only been born a couple of weeks, and he makes more noise than she does already.'

'Are you gypsies?' Harry asked.

The man laughed. 'Gypsies, tinkers, they call us plenty of things. We're travellers, boy. Keep ourselves to ourselves. Don't ask no favours and we don't expect none.' The girl came running back and gave the old man a bottle. He opened it and smelt it. 'Well done, Meg. You know what to do, don't you?'

The girl knelt down beside Harry and poured some lotion onto his ankle and then she began to rub it in. It was cold at first and Harry drew in his breath sharply.

'Gentle now,' said the old man. 'Gentle at first, there's a girl. That's a nasty ankle he's got.'

The girl never looked up all the time she was working on his ankle. She even ignored Ocky when she came back and sniffed at Harry's foot. Ocky climbed on Harry's knee to watch her. Whether it was the lotion in the bottle or the strength of her fingers Harry did not know. All he knew was that even as she rubbed his ankle, somehow the pain of it was being drawn out of him.

'Rollo,' said the old man. 'Go and hang those rabbits up, and whilst you're about it you can make us all some nice hot tea. You hungry are you, boy?' Harry nodded.

'And Ocky's always hungry,' he said.

'Ocky?'

'The chimpanzee. She eats anything,' Harry said.

'We've got bread to spare, haven't we? We've always got bread.'

The tea was hot and sweet. Harry warmed his hands around the mug and watched Ocky devour her bread.

Rollo threw more wood on the fire and they all huddled closer to it, sipping their tea in silence. The girl's fingers only paused to pour more lotion over his ankle and then she'd start again, the same rhythm, on and on.

The old man was lighting up his pipe. "Course,' he said, ''course you don't have to tell us what you don't want to tell us, boy. But you've set us all wondering a bit about what brought you here, you and the monkey, in the middle of the night. 'Course we're used to being woken up in the middle of the night. Zak over there, that's him with the violin – he's my oldest boy – he's often had a skinful at the pub and come back and woken us up playing his blessed fiddle. Nothing new in that, but it's not every night we wake up to find a monkey in the camp, let alone a stranger like yourself. You're not from hereabouts, are you?'

'London,' said Harry.

'London, eh? Well you're a long way from home, aren't you, boy?' said the old man.

'I'm running away,' said Harry. He was too tired to lie, and anyway he sensed they wouldn't believe any story except the true story, and for some reason he very much wanted them to believe him. So he told them everything. They asked no questions but sat looking at him in rapt silence. Only Ocky was inattentive. To begin

135

with she was happy grooming herself on Harry's lap but when she started on his hair he pushed her off. She complained bitterly and sulked by the fire for some minutes. Then she came back and sat by the little girl who was pulling Harry's sock back on. Ocky put her arm around the girl's shoulder and explored her face with her fingers. She didn't seem to mind one bit. None of all this seemed to distract the listeners.

'You're still a bit of a way from Bournemouth,' said Rollo when Harry had finished. 'It's a good twenty miles from here to the sea and Bournemouth's another ten after that.'

'I can walk it,' said Harry.

'Not with that foot you can't,' said Rollo. 'He'd best stay here for a bit, eh, Pa?'

The old man stood up and pulled the blanket round his shoulders. 'I'm not saying anything one way or the other, not till the morning. I've got a lot to think over and I'm going to sleep on it. There's room in our caravan, Rollo. You can bring the boy and the monkey to sleep with us tonight and we'll talk about all this in the morning. And Zak, if you start up with that fiddle of yours again, I'll throw it in the fire, you see if I won't. Now let's all get some sleep.' Clearly no one argued with the old man for everyone dispersed at once to their caravans, the baby's mother smiling at Harry as she went.

Rollo took Harry by the arm and helped him up the steps into the caravan. It was warm inside and smelt of oil. There wasn't much room to move about. Ocky explored the place quickly and came back to the bed. The old man said nothing more to anyone but pulled a blanket over his shoulders and blew out the lamp. Harry and Rollo slept head to foot on the same bed with Ocky curled up in between. She was asleep before any of them, breathing heavily in the dark beside them. Harry tried to say his prayers as he knew he should, but he kept thinking of the girl instead. He could still feel her fingers on his ankle. He was wondering how someone who looked so fragile – every part of her was tiny – could have such strong hands and could run that fast. He was still only halfway through his prayers when he fell asleep.

He woke with a start, conscious of cold air on his face. It was light and the door of the caravan was open behind him. He looked about him. He was quite alone. He sat up and was about to call for Ocky when he saw her through the door. She was squatting by the fire with a crust of bread in her hand and with one arm around the girl. She was kneeling beside her and bathing Ocky's hand, dabbing gently at the cut and talking softly to her. And then he heard Rollo, his voice raised in anger.

'And I'm telling you, Zak, you can't do it.'

'Don't know why not. It's worth a pretty penny, I should think,' said Zak. 'After all, it came from a circus didn't it? He told us so didn't he? Proper trained up, that's what he said. We've got to make a decent living, haven't we? We won't hardly get rich sharpening knives and making a few clothes pegs, will we?'

'That's enough, the two of you,' said the old man. 'Always at each other's throats you are, always have been. Your mother – God rest her – she'd be ashamed of the both of you, she would.' Harry was at the door of the caravan by now and the old man had seen him. 'Ah there you are, boy,' he said. 'Take no notice of Zak, he's just talking. He doesn't mean it.' Harry hesitated at the top of the steps. 'Don't you go worrying yourself about it. No one's going to sell your monkey. Come on down. We've got some tea for you, and you can have some jam on your bread – rosehip jelly. Mary there, my daughter-in-law, she makes the best jam in the world, don't you, Mary girl?' Harry supposed Mary must be the mother of the girl as well as the baby. 'Your foot better is it?' the old man asked as Harry came down the steps. He nodded. It was still tender and felt weak when he put any weight on it, but at least the pain was gone. The piece of bread and jam Rollo gave him when he sat down was so big you needed two hands to hold it. And the old man was right, the rosehip jelly *was* the best jam in the world.

'Well,' said the old man coming to sit down beside him. 'I've told them straight what I've been thinking, boy, and now I'll tell you. I've been thinking most of the night. You don't sleep so well when you get older.' He seemed unwilling to go on. 'Well, what I've been thinking is this. We'd like to help you, boy, honest we would: but there's one or two things you've got to understand. If I've learned anything over the years it's that you've got to look after your own, your own kind I mean. You don't understand what I mean, do you, boy? You see there's two different worlds – there's your world out there and then there's the gypsy world. There's people in your world that don't much care for us. They don't like how we live because we don't live like they do. We don't believe in the same things, see. That's just how it is, how it has been and how it always will be. Now, it seems to me that they'll be out looking for you, boy; and whatever else they are they're not stupid. It won't take them long to track you down. If they find you here with us, boy, we're in trouble; and they won't just move us on like they usually do. We're used to that. You've heard the stories about us, have you?'

'Stories?' said Harry, shaking his head.

'Well, there's some people who won't let their children out of their houses when we're about. And do you know why? Because they're frightened we'll kidnap them. No, it's true, and that's what they'd say, boy, if they found you here. They'd say that we kidnapped you and then where'd we be? You understand what I'm saying, boy? I've got to look after my own, like I said.'

Harry still wasn't sure what he meant.

'What Pa's saying,' said Zak, with some impatience, 'is that you can't stay here. You got to go. You got a home to go to, haven't you? Not our fault you ran off, is it?'

'But he doesn't want to go back home, does he?' said Rollo. 'And if he does, you heard what he said, they'll take Ocky away from him.'

'Should have thought of that before, shouldn't he?' said Zak. 'If I had my way we'd sell the monkey and turn the boy in like I said. Maybe there's a reward, you never know.'

'There'll be none of that,' said the old man firmly. 'But the boy's got to go, that's all there is to it.'

'We can't do it, Pa,' Mary said quietly. 'We can't just

send him away.' She stood up and brought a mug of tea over to Harry, and then looked down at the old man. 'You know we can't,' she said. 'Look at him, he can't hardly walk, can he? And anyway, what would he do out there on his own? He'll be safe here for a time at least, till his foot gets a bit better. No one's going to find him here unless we tell them, and we're not likely to tell anyone are we?'

'That's right, Pa,' said Rollo. 'No one'll know. No one'll find him here.'

The old man thought for some moments and then looked up at Mary and smiled. 'Lot of sense in what you say, Mary girl; there always is,' he said. 'All right. The boy stays, but only till his foot gets better and no one says a word, you hear me, Zak? Don't you go telling anyone in that pub. I know what you're like when you get some drink inside you.' He turned to Harry wagging his finger at him. 'But I'll tell you one thing for nothing, boy: you were honest with us and I'll be honest with you. You didn't ought to have done what you did, and you know it. A boy your age belongs with his mother and that monkey belongs with that circus man, you know he does. You got to think about your mother, boy; and you've got to think about the circus man.'

But Harry had little time that morning to think

about anything. Whilst he finished his tea Ocky and the girl chased each other round and round the fire. She could dodge and twist fast enough to make a real game of it, and Ocky loved it. Whenever she got bored with it the girl threw her some bread or a turnip. It seemed she liked chasing turnips more than eating bread. Rollo and Harry watched them playing for a bit and then Rollo tapped him on the shoulder.

'Got something to show you,' he said. He took him behind his caravan where there were hens scratching at the ground in amongst some old tyres and rusting scrap metal. Rollo pointed. There was a little corrugated shed up against the hedge with a blanket for a door. Rollo lifted it up and there stood a motorbike with a sidecar.

'Does it work?' Harry asked.

''Course it does,' said Rollo cuffing him playfully. 'I'll give you a go later; but I've got to change the oil first. Give me a hand, will you?' And they wheeled it out into the open. It was all gleaming black and glittering silver. 'It's a Triumph,' said Rollo, patting it proudly, 'except I made the sidecar myself.'

They changed the oil and cleaned the plugs, and all the time Rollo explained the intricacies of the engine and why this and that made his Triumph, without doubt, the best bike in the entire world. 'You can sit on it now if you like,' Rollo said and he helped him up. Harry felt like a king up there astride it. He was savouring the moment when Ocky suddenly appeared scattering the squawking chickens in all directions. She leapt up onto the handlebars first and then onto his shoulder and then down into the sidecar. When Rollo went off to fetch a spanner she went with him, holding his hand. Harry felt a pang of disappointment at how easily Ocky made friends with everyone. He'd been left to polish the fuel tank. 'Just breathe on it and rub,' Rollo had told him as he'd handed him a cloth, and he was doing just that when he noticed Meg coming towards him. She was holding the baby over her shoulder.

'We haven't got a name for him yet,' she said. 'Mum says I've got to burp him. You can pat him on the back if you like, it's good for him. He gets a bellyache else.' Harry tapped the baby gently.

'I've got one like that,' he said, 'he's called Georgie.'

'Harder than that,' she said, tutting at him. 'Here, you hold him, I'll pat him.' She handed Harry the baby and showed him how to hold his hand behind the baby's head to support it. 'It flops around if you don't,' she said. Harry felt the skin of the baby's cheek against his.

'He smells of milk,' he said.

'Not always he doesn't,' she said, and they laughed together. It was the first time her face had lost its seriousness. Harry decided she was pretty when she smiled, very pretty. 'Watch. If you put your finger in his fist he grips it. He won't let go. Like a little bulldog he is.' The burp came at last and the dribbles with it. 'That's done it,' she said. 'Come on, we can give him back to Mum now.'

Her mother was sitting on the steps of the caravan skinning a rabbit. 'Time for his rest,' she said. 'You can put him in his cradle if you like,' and Meg carried the baby past her and up into the caravan. Harry did not like to look at the rabbit, but he found it difficult not to. Mary saw it and chuckled. 'That's the trouble with you people,' she said, 'you wrap yourselves up against the world. You only see what you want to see, and you don't understand much of that. It's only a dead rabbit, Harry. It won't hurt you none.'

Meg came running down the steps. 'Done it,' she said, and she took Harry's hand and turned to go.

'Don't go near the village,' Mary called after her. 'We don't want any more trouble, do we?'

'What does she mean?' Harry asked as they ran off through the trees. No one had held hands with him since he was little, except for crossing roads.

'They don't like us up in the village,' she said. 'They throw stones at us.'

'What do you do?' Harry asked.

'Throw them back,' she said and she smiled. Harry noticed she was fingering a necklace of large nut-brown beads.

They wandered off hand in hand into the field of tanks, and then she pulled him sharply behind one of them and let go of his hand. She peered round the side of the tank. 'I've got to be sure no one's following us,' she said.

'What about Ocky?' Harry said. He hadn't even thought of her until then.

'Uncle Rollo will look after her, or Mum will,' she said. 'I've got a secret, something no one else knows except me. You can only see it if you promise never to tell.'

'Cross my heart,' said Harry. She seemed satisfied with that, took his hand again and they walked on.

'I've got a tank of my very own,' she said and she pointed ahead of her. 'That one, the one without a gun.'

Except for its missing gun it looked like every other tank in the field. To Harry they all looked even more wrecked and battered in the light of day. She jumped up onto it with no difficulty – just like Ocky, Harry thought

– and then she helped him up after her. 'I mended your foot, didn't I?' she said. She didn't wait for an answer but waggled her fingers in his face. 'I knew I could. I've got the healing touch. That's what Grandpa says.' She lifted up the tank turret, lowered it gently and let herself down. 'You coming?' she called up at him. Harry peered in. The girl was standing below him ankle deep in straw. 'You can't see from up there. You've got to come down.' Harry sat on the edge, turned round and lowered himself until his feet touched the straw. 'Careful where you walk,' she said gripping his arm tightly. 'I've got eleven now.'

'Eleven what?'

'Hedgehogs. I'm going to have a hundred soon. I like Uncle Rollo, but he's a pig sometimes. He knows where they all go to hide in winter see, and he brings them back to cook them.' Harry made a face. 'That's what I think,' said Meg. 'They cook them in mud to make the prickles fall off. But I've found out where he puts them, so I rescue them, and bring them here where he can't find them ever again.' She crouched down and brushed aside the straw until she found one, curled up in a ball. 'I won't wake him,' she said. 'Wouldn't be right. They sleep right through the winter, you know.' She clambered over and sat down in the driver's seat. 'And

I've got apples, too.' And she reached down under the seat and held up a wooden bowl full of apples. 'We'll share one.' They took one bite each and handed it back and forth until it was finished except for the core.

'Can I keep the core?' said Harry. 'Ocky likes the cores.' Meg gave it to him.

'I think someone was killed in this tank, don't you?' she said looking around her. 'It's all busted up. They're all busted up. I come here at night sometimes and I'm sure there's ghosts in here then. I can feel them all around me.'

'I saw some sheep last night,' said Harry lightly. 'Didn't see any ghosts.'

'No, I mean it,' she said and she was quite serious. 'I've talked to them. They're listening, I know they are.'

Harry didn't like the thought of it – it made him feel strange. He changed the subject. 'What're they all here for, all these tanks?'

She shrugged her shoulders. 'Scrap, I suppose. Not much use for anything else, are they?' And she looked at him. 'You told us last night, you said your father got killed. Have you ever seen his ghost? Does he come back sometimes to see you?'

''Course not,' said Harry. 'I don't need to see him. I can remember him, can't I? Want to see his medal? I've got it here.' And he fumbled in his trouser pocket until he found it and then put it into her hand. She looked down at it.

'What's it say on it?'

'*For Courage*. It's a Distinguished Flying Medal,' said Harry.

'What's that mean?'

'It means he was brave,' said Harry.

'I'm brave sometimes,' said Meg. 'You should see my dad when he's drunk, but I'm not frightened of him, don't care how drunk he gets. When he plays the violin he's all right, but sometimes he has a go at Mum instead and he hits her. I try to stop him. I'm not frightened of him, honest I'm not.' She pushed the tears off her cheek. 'It's pretty this is, like a sort of brooch isn't it? And it's got a pin in it too. Can I wear it?' Harry helped to pin it on her cardigan.

'Does he hit you sometimes too?' Harry asked.

She nodded and patted the medal on her chest. 'Sometimes,' she said. 'Looks nice doesn't it? Who's the man on it?'

'That's the king,' Harry said, trying to disguise the surprise in his voice. He thought everyone knew what the king looked like.

She twisted the medal around and was looking at the

king's face. 'I can't read,' she said suddenly. 'I can't read and I can't write.'

'Don't you go to school?' Harry asked. She shook her head.

'I went to school for two weeks once, but I didn't like it. They kept calling me a dirty tinker so I don't go any more. But you could teach me though, couldn't you? You could teach me to read?'

'I'll try,' said Harry, 'but I'm not that good myself.'

''Course you are,' she said. 'I've got books, lots of them and they've got pictures in, too.' He followed her to the back of the tank treading carefully through the straw. She was crouching by an open box. 'They're always crawling into it,' she said laughing and she lifted a hedgehog out and buried it deep in the straw. There were four books inside the box, all of them stained and torn. 'Grandpa gave them to me,' she said. Harry picked out the only book that he knew, *Mike Mulligan and his Steam Shovel*, and they sat down side by side in the straw.

He did it the way his mother had taught him. First he read a sentence right through, and then with a finger under each word he made her repeat the words after him again and again until she began to recognise them. The lesson was intense and she learnt fast. It was as if she was trying to catch up in a few short hours on all the teaching she had missed. If ever she got a word wrong, she would become very upset; but through it all she stayed grimly determined. They were only half way through the book when they heard Mary calling her from far away. She slammed the book shut at once and put it back in the box. 'We'll come back later, shall we?' she said. 'Come on, quick. I don't want them to come looking for us. If they find this place they'll eat all the hedgehogs and my dad will burn the books. He hates books, but it's only because he can't read himself.'

They could smell lunch from far off. By the time they got there Ocky was already helping herself from the enamel bowl she'd been given. The old man sat beside her tickling the top of her head and laughing. 'She likes her rabbit stew,' he said. Harry hated the idea of eating rabbits, and tried to swallow the first mouthful without tasting it; but he did taste it in spite of himself, and like Meg beside him he didn't finish till he'd wiped off every trace of gravy with his bread.

He had gathered Ocky into his lap and was letting her lick his fingers when they heard the motorbike.

'That'll be Rollo come back,' said the old man. 'Him and that bike of his. I've told him time and time again he should pay more attention to the horses and caravans, or sharpen a few more knives. But no, not young Rollo, he does as he pleases, that one.'

'Times are changing, Pa,' said Mary.

'Too fast for me, Mary girl,' said the old man, shaking his head. 'Too fast for all of us if you ask me.'

The bike came bouncing down the rutty track that led down into the camp from the road. Rollo leapt off and ran towards them. 'Quick,' he shouted. 'They're coming!'

'What do you mean? Who's coming?' said the old man getting to his feet. Ocky clung tighter to Harry's neck.

'Zak's gone and done it.' Rollo was breathing hard. 'I knew he would. You can't tell him anything. Up in the pub he was, with his fiddle. Playing tunes for his drinks, just like he always does. I heard him, Pa. He's told them. He's told them all about the boy and the monkey. Of course they didn't believe him, so what does Zak do? He goes and takes a bet with them. "Five bob says I'm right", he tells them. "Come and see for yourselves, lads" he says. And that's just what they're doing. They're on their way now in the landlord's van and they're only just behind me.'

CHAPTER NINE

'GET THEM OUT OF HERE, QUICK,' THE OLD MAN said softly. Harry picked Ocky up and ran away through the trees as best he could after Rollo and Meg. Already they could hear the van slowing down as it turned off the road, and came bumping and rattling down the track. Then the wheels were spinning and the engine was revving angrily. Harry's ankle was too weak to go any faster, and Meg saw it and came back for him. She took his hand and they ran out ofthe trees into the field of tanks and hid with Rollo behind the first one they came to. Harry peered over the tank track he was leaning on and saw the glass of the van's windscreen glinting through the trees.

'Don't you come back till I call you,' Rollo whispered. 'Find yourself somewhere to hide.'

'Where?' said Meg.

'What about your hedgehog tank,' Rollo said, and he smiled knowingly. 'They won't find you there just so long as you don't make any noise. Can you keep Ocky quiet, Harry?' Harry nodded.

'Hope so,' he said.

'So do I,' said Rollo, 'because if they find you we're all for it, you and us both.'

As he turned to go Meg clutched at his arm. 'You know about my hedgehogs, then?' she said.

'Course I do,' Rollo said.

'And my books?'

Rollo nodded.

'You won't tell, will you?'

'I got to go,' said Rollo, trying to pull his arm free.

'Promise me, Uncle Rollo,' she insisted fiercely.

'Promise,' said Rollo and he was gone, bending over and running low along the line of tanks. They watched him as he skirted round the trees and appeared at last from behind the old man's caravan. The doors of the van were opening now and there was the sound of raised voices, Zak's amongst them. Harry saw the old man get up and go to meet them, Rollo at his side. Then Meg was tugging at his hand and they were running through the field of tanks, Ocky clinging to his neck.

It wasn't easy getting Ocky into the tank. Harry didn't dare let her go in case she ran off, so he tried to hand her up to Meg but she was far too heavy to lift that high. In the end he had to clamber up with Ocky hanging onto his back, her arms around his throat. By the time he lowered himself down into the tank he was almost choked. Meg came down after them shutting the lid behind her. She crouched down in the straw beside him.

'The hedgehogs,' she whispered. 'What if she sees the hedgehogs?' Harry had already thought of that, and hugged Ocky tight to him as he crawled carefully through and up into the driver's seat. If she spotted a hedgehog Harry knew only too well the whooping and shrieking that would inevitably follow. The girl climbed in beside him and Ocky took the two apples she offered her eagerly.

'Only got six more,' she said, watching Ocky take her first huge bite. She would only sit still for as long as it took to finish the apples and Harry wondered if that would be long enough.

'He knew,' whispered the girl.

'Who?'

'Uncle Rollo. He knew all along about this place, all about my hedgehogs. If he tells my dad about my books he'll burn them, I know he will.'

There was a rustle in the straw behind them and Ocky climbed up on Harry's shoulder to look, hooting with excitement. Harry acted quickly. He snatched one of her apples and dropped it on his lap to distract her. It worked. She jumped down at once and retrieved it. *'Va bene,'* he said, and stroked her head. *'Va bene.'* She offered him a taste but Harry was careful to take only a small bite. She'd almost finished one of them already, and he had no idea how long they would be there, how long the apples would have to last.

They sat in the silent darkness of the tank and listened, dreading the sound of approaching voices. Long minutes went by and they thought the danger might be over. They hoped too soon. Ocky had eaten the fifth apple when they heard a cough and then voices, faint at first but coming closer and strident with anger. *'Va bene*, Ocky,' Harry whispered. *'Va bene. Va bene.'*

'And I'm telling you,' it was Zak talking, 'that I know a g'rilla when I see one, and I know a boy when I see one, and I'm telling you they were in the camp.'

'So you say, Zak. So you say,' came another voice from amongst the mocking laughter. 'But we've looked everywhere haven't we? We think you've been seeing things again, things that aren't there, 'lucinations they call it, don't they. It'll be elephants next, pink ones, and giraffes.' There was more laughter and then Zak's voice was shouting.

'She's with them, I know she is. That ruddy girl of mine, she's run off with them, hidden them away somewhere. Took a shine to the boy she did. She's out here somewhere. She's always off on her own and I've seen her going this way. Meg!' he bellowed. 'Meg! You come back, you hear me? I'll give you the hiding of your life, I will.'

'She ran off because she's frightened, that's all Zak,' said Rollo. 'What do you expect when you come home drunk all the time?' They were right beside the tank now. 'It was the drink like they say, making you see things. There was no gorilla, Zak, and there was no boy. I mean I'd have noticed them wouldn't I? And I've had nothing to drink, have I? I say there's no gorilla. Pa says there's no gorilla. Mary says there's no gorilla. What more do you want, eh?'

'He's right, Zak,' said someone else. 'I'm not going to spend all afternoon looking for a gorilla that isn't there. Five bob you bet me, Zak, and you've lost. All you got to do is pay up, and then we can all go back and have a drink.'

They could hear Zak muttering and complaining as they began to walk away. Harry had held his breath as long as he could and let it out slowly now. He felt Meg's hand grip his in the darkness and he squeezed it; and then from behind them in the tank came a loud snoring noise. Alarmed, Ocky stiffened in Harry's lap and stopped eating her apples. The footsteps were coming back towards them.

'Back there it was,' said Zak. 'I heard something. I know I did. Listen!' And once again it came, a deep rhythmic snore from under the straw. 'I told you. I told you,' said Zak, 'it's in here, in this one.' And he banged the side of the tank with his stick.

Rollo laughed. 'No gorilla in there, Zak,' he said. 'That's my hedgehog tank, that is. I keep them in there: fatten 'em up I do. It's like a sort of hedgehog farm. I've got dozens of them in there. Fatten them up and eat them. Roast them in clay in the fire. Delicious, they are.'

Amidst the laughter they could hear groans of disgust and disbelief. 'You don't believe me, eh?' said Rollo. 'I'll show you, then.' They heard feet clambering up on the tank, and then the turret was open and Rollo's face was there looking down at them. Meg knew what to do at once without being asked. She rummaged around in the straw, and a few moments later she had a hedgehog curled up in her hands. Rollo reached down and took it. He winked at her and at Harry, and then he

157

was gone again. 'See?' he said, and the lid banged down shutting out the light. 'Hedgehogs, just like I said. I've got dozens more in there.'

'Prickly sort of gorilla, eh Zak?' said someone, and they walked away laughing, Zak still protesting loudly that he knew the difference between a hedgehog and a gorilla.

They waited until they heard the van start up in the distance. They couldn't have waited any longer anyway because Ocky had finished all the apples by now, and was becoming more and more interested in the snoring from the straw behind her. It was all Harry could do to hang on to her as he climbed out. They meant to stay by the tank until Rollo called them, but Ocky took matters into her own hands. For just a moment Harry's grip on her hand slackened and she broke free of him, scampering away and out of sight. Meg went after her leaving Harry to find his own way back to the campfire. When he got there Ocky was stalking around the fire on two legs, a stick in her hand, hooting exultantly. Mary was coming down the steps of the caravan, the baby in her arms. 'He didn't mean it,' she said, shaking her head. 'He never means it.'

'All right, is he?' Rollo asked.

'Dead to the world now,' she said, and Harry thought she'd been crying. 'Nothing will wake him now, not until the pub opens tonight.' And she sighed deeply.

'I told you,' said the old man. 'You can't say I didn't warn you. There's times you don't like to be right.' No one spoke. 'We can't take the risk, not any more we can't. If the drink's talked once then it'll talk again; and sooner or later someone's going to see the monkey or hear it, and they'll put two and two together.' He looked up at Rollo. 'I'm sorry, Rollo, but they got to go; and now, before it's too late.' He turned to Harry. 'You understand me don't you, boy? We haven't got no choice, not any more. Nothing else we can do. Like I told you, I've got to look after my own.' He looked down and banged his pipe on the log he was sitting on. 'You'd best take your monkey, and be off back home where you belong.' Mary tried to protest but the old man would have none of it this time. 'They've got to go,' he said. His mind was made up and there was no changing it.

'Well, I'm not going home again,' said Harry. 'I'm not.'

The old man looked up at him sharply. 'Where you go is your own business, boy; but I want you gone from here, you hear me?'

'Then I'll take him, Pa,' said Rollo. 'If he's got to go, I'll take him on my bike. I've got room for him and Ocky. They can go in the sidecar.'

Until this moment Meg had said nothing. She'd stood watching them impassively, but now she ran over to her grandfather and pleaded with him, her arms around his knees. 'Let him stay, Grandpa,' she said. 'Oh, please.' The old man pushed her away gently. 'Please. He's teaching me to read, Grandpa. I know some words already, don't I, Harry? Please, Grandpa, please.' The old man got up and walked slowly away. She appealed to her mother then, but Mary turned away from her shaking her head. 'It's no good, Meg,' she said. Meg ran off into the trees, her arm over her eyes. Rollo went after her and when he came back a few moments later he came back alone.

Ocky fitted snugly on the floor of the sidecar. They made her a bed of straw which she arranged to her own satisfaction before sitting down at Harry's feet. It needed several kicks for Rollo to bring the machine to life. The old man lifted his head as the bike moved away, his face swathed in pipe smoke. Mary waved the baby's hand and smiled sadly at Harry. Meg was nowhere to be seen. Harry kept his eyes on the trees hoping she would come back to see him off, but she didn't.

At the end of the rutty track Rollo looked down at him. 'Where to, Harry?' he said. 'London or Bournemouth?'

'Bournemouth,' said Harry, and he felt Ocky trying

to climb up his legs. He pushed her down gently. '*Va bene*, Ocky,' he said. '*Va bene,*' and although she tried again and again to crawl up onto his lap her determination diminished as the journey went on. She eventually settled for her bread and her turnip, and curled up in the straw.

Talking was quite impossible as the bike roared along but Rollo winked and smiled at him from time to time.

The exhilaration of the cold wind on his face had quickly blown away much of the shock and sadness he had felt at leaving Meg behind so suddenly. He was wondering if he'd ever see her again when the engine spluttered and coughed and died. He heard Rollo cursing and then they were cruising silently to a halt at the side of the road. Rollo told him to stay where he was and to look after Ocky. He didn't want her jumping out and running around on the road, he said. He tinkered anxiously with the engine, muttering on about oil filters and plugs and carburettors, all of which he'd explained to Harry that morning but whose functions Harry had already forgotten. After some minutes he straightened up and wiped his hands with a dirty rag.

'Should do the trick,' he said, and he pushed the rag into his pocket. 'Oh, I nearly forgot. Meg told me to give you this. She said it was yours.' It was the medal.

Harry had quite forgotten she'd had it. He had not even missed it. 'And this as well,' Rollo said, 'she wants you to keep it, for luck.' It was the necklace of dark brown beads that Meg had worn. 'Oak apples they are,' said Rollo, putting it over Harry's head. 'I found them for her but she made it herself. Always brought her good luck, she said.'

A black car was coming towards them. It had slowed almost to a stop before Harry realised it was a police car. The window wound down.

'In some sort of trouble, are you?' said the policeman looking from Harry to Rollo and back again.

'Not any more,' said Rollo. 'Fixed it.'

'Nice machine,' said the policeman. Ocky shifted at Harry's feet and Harry felt her hands on his knees. He pushed her down. 'Triumph, isn't it?'

Rollo patted the petrol tank and swung his leg over. 'Not another one like it,' he said.

'Cold in that sidecar is it, son?' the policeman was looking at him hard and Harry had to look away.

'Bit shy my brother is,' said Rollo.

'What's that thing around your neck?' laughed the policeman.

'Oak apples,' said Harry.

'Doesn't look much like apples to me,' said the

162

policeman and he wound up his window and drove off laughing.

'See?' said Rollo smiling. 'She was right, wasn't she? It is a lucky necklace.'

Ocky was wide awake now and offering Harry her turnip. Harry offered it to Rollo who wrinkled his nose. 'Not on your nelly,' he said, 'but thanks anyway.' It was starting to rain. Rollo looked up. 'Better get you there before you get soaked,' he said. 'We'll be in Bournemouth in ten minutes, 'long as it doesn't break down again. You know the way to go, do you?'

Harry told him to go to the pier, from there he would know the way to Seaview Terrace, he thought. It all looked just the same to Harry as they drove along the promenade from the pier, except that the sea and the sky were grey now and there was hardly anyone on the beach, only a dog or two prancing in the shallows and a solitary walker in a raincoat, hands behind his back, walking past the spot where Harry's sandcastle had been. Rollo stopped opposite number twenty-two and turned off the engine.

'You sure this is it, Harry?' he said. Harry was certain it was the right house but the balconies were red now, not green as he had remembered them. The front garden was smaller than he'd thought and there was no swing in it either. He was sure there'd been a swing in the front garden. He lifted Ocky out and stroked her head. *'Va bene, va bene,'* he said softly.

'What's that mean?' Rollo asked, 'you're always saying it to him.'

'Don't know really,' said Harry. 'She likes it, that's all I know, and it calms her down. Don't know what it means, though.'

'Miss her, we will,' said Rollo, 'and you. But we'll be keeping a bit of you.'

'What do you mean?'

'Didn't she tell you?'

'Tell me what?' said Harry.

'Meg and Mary, they decided about the baby. They're calling him Harry.'

Harry was so full of things to say he couldn't bring himself to say anything except a mumbled thankyou; then holding Ocky's hand he crossed the road. At the gate to number twenty-two he turned. 'I like your Triumph,' he said; and Rollo smiled and waved.

'Best bike in the world,' he said.

Harry took a deep breath and banged the knocker. Beside him Ocky picked at a plant in a pot and was tasting it when the door opened. For some moments Aunty Ivy stood staring at Ocky. She was swallowing hard and her face was flushed. Harry remembered the scarf she was wearing.

'It's me,' said Harry.

''Course it's you, pet,' she said, reaching out and touching his cheek, her eyes still fixed on Ocky. 'But what's that?'

'That's Ocky,' said Harry. 'She's a chimpanzee. She won't hurt you.'

'You sure?'

'I'm sure,' Harry said. 'She's just like us. So long as she knows you like her, she'll like you.' Aunty Ivy looked past them down the road.

'Your mother with you, is she?' she said. Harry shook his head.

'We've run away, Aunty Ivy,' he said. 'Ocky and me, we've run away.'

'You'd better come in out of the rain,' said Aunty Ivy putting an arm around him.

In the warmth of the hall she took off his coat. 'Look at the state of you,' she said, brushing his hair off his forehead. Harry heard the bike start up in the street outside and listened until he could hear it no more. She smiled down at him. 'I'm glad you came to me, pet,' she said and she put her arms around him and hugged him to her. 'What you need is a nice hot cup of cocoa.'

Inside it was all just as Harry remembered it. The three ducks flying up the wall, the tall ticking clock with a ship sailing past the moon on the face of it, and the smell he'd found nowhere else, a mixture of furniture polish and lavender and Aunty Ivy's cooking.

Ocky made for the stairs at once and had to be retrieved, which wasn't easy because if you chased her, as Harry did, she swung out over the banisters or scampered up onto the landing. Aunty Ivy was clearly worried, Harry could see that.

'Have you anything she could eat?' Harry said. 'She likes fruit, or bread, maybe?'

'I baked some this morning,' she said and ran into the kitchen. She came back in a moment or two, a crust in her hand. Harry enticed Ocky down the stairs with it. '*Va bene, va bene*,' he said, and Ocky needed no further invitation. She sat on the kitchen floor eating her crust while Harry drank down his cocoa and ate his biscuits, digestive biscuits just like they always were. He told her everything from start to finish, even about the gypsies. He knew he could trust Aunty Ivy completely. She wouldn't tell anybody, he was sure of that.

When he'd finished Aunty Ivy said nothing. She took the mugs to the sink and began to wash them up. 'So that's why we came here, Aunty Ivy,' said Harry.

'You said I could come and stay anytime, didn't you. You said so, didn't you?'

'Of course I did, pet,' said Aunty Ivy.

'You see, Ocky,' said Harry triumphantly, 'I said she'd look after us. I told you.' He could see that Ocky was intrigued by the sound of the tap running into the sink. She jumped up onto a chair so that she could see better. Harry knew what she was going to do but was too slow to stop her. She bounded across the floor and sprang up onto the draining board. Perhaps if Aunty Ivy had not screamed there would have been just a broken glass or two, but as it was she let out a piercing yell. Shrieking with terror, Ocky leapt from the sink, scattering glasses and crockery in all directions and sending a glass fruit bowl rolling slowly along the worktop. It seemed to hover for a moment on the edge and then fell, crashing to the floor. Aunty Ivy, her hands still at her mouth, had turned quite pale. When she tried to speak she seemed unable to find her voice.

'She didn't mean it,' said Harry. 'Honest she didn't.' He held out his hand to Ocky and offered his digestive biscuit. *'Va bene*, Ocky. *Va bene.'* Ocky came out of her corner slowly and ran around the kitchen keeping her distance from Aunty Ivy. She climbed whimpering onto Harry's lap and buried her face in his jumper. 'I'm sorry,

Aunty Ivy,' Harry said. He could see there were tears in her eyes as she bent down to pick up the pieces. 'She gets a bit excited sometimes but she didn't mean any harm, honest she didn't.'

'I know that, pet,' said Aunty Ivy. 'I shouldn't have screamed, that's all. I just couldn't help myself.' She looked up and tried to smile through her tears. 'It doesn't matter. I'll tidy this up right away. We don't want her cutting her feet, do we? Now you go on upstairs, take the monkey with you, and have a nice hot bath. We can't have you catching cold, can we? Have a good long soak, pet. Fill it right up. There's plenty of hot water.'

In the bathroom Harry moved all the bottles and brushes and mugs out of Ocky's reach before he ran the bath. He filled it almost to the top and then lay back and revelled in the warmth of it. Ocky seemed nervous at first. She squatted for some time on the lavatory seat, watching him in the bath and scratching herself. Occasionally she would lean over and touch the water with her fingertips and taste it. It took several minutes before she plucked up enough courage to come and stand by the bath. She tasted the soap and didn't like it. She dipped her hand in the bath and drank from it, and then she began to pat the water, only gently at first; but patting soon turned to slapping, and she was soon jumping up and down and hooting with delight as the water slurped and splashed over the side. Harry could not stop her now. By the time she'd finished much of the bathwater was on the floor and she had soaked herself to the skin. Harry let the plug out before she could do any more damage and then mopped up the floor with the bathmat as best he could. He had quite a tussle with her to recover his towel and then his clothes, but at last he was dried and dressed and ready to go downstairs. He crouched down in front of Ocky, rubbing her with a towel.

'You've got to behave, Ocky,' he said. 'If you go on like this she won't let us stay.' Ocky pulled the towel out of his hand and threw it on the ground. She did not want to be dried. 'You must be good, Ocky. You must be.' Ocky looked away from him. 'You want to stay here, don't you Ocky?' Harry said and he stroked her head. 'We've got nowhere else to go. You've got to be good. *Va bene, va bene.*'

And Ocky was good, as good as Harry had ever seen her. Aunty Ivy seemed a little anxious, he thought, when they first went downstairs, but once Ocky was settled in a chair with a biscuit she seemed a little happier. Harry saw that all the ornaments had been put away on the top shelf, as well as the radio which was turned on now. Ocky looked up at it and hooted softly from time to time.

'She likes music,' said Harry, 'specially violins. It's because of Mr Nobody – you know, the clown at the circus I was telling you about. He played the violin, remember? And so did Zak at the gypsy camp.' Aunty Ivy nodded and smiled nervously. She sat down beside him on the sofa and read him a story, several stories. She had remembered that *Just So Stories* was his favourite book, but what she didn't know, of course, was that Harry could read quite well on his own now. He never said anything, though. When she'd finished 'The Cat that Walked by Itself' she put her arm around him and kissed him on the head. 'Bit like you, that cat,' she said. 'Going off on your own like that, walking on your wild lone.'

'I wasn't alone,' said Harry, 'I was with Ocky. Look at her, Aunty Ivy.' Ocky was curled up fast asleep in the armchair under the radio. 'I'll make a cup of tea for us, shall I?' said Aunty Ivy, looking at her watch.

She was still in the kitchen making the tea when Harry heard a car come to a stop outside the house. A car door slammed, waking Ocky with a start. She came over to the sofa and sat down on Harry's lap, still sleepy.

Harry took no more notice, not until he heard the front door click open. He went over to the window. Aunty Ivy was standing at the gate talking to someone. It was dark outside now and difficult to see who it was at first.

Aunty Ivy was talking. 'It's been ages since I phoned you,' she said. 'What kept you?' And then Harry heard who it was that she was talking to.

'I'm sorry, Mrs Coleman.' It was Bill's voice. 'Terrible traffic jam coming out of London. Where is he, then?'

'Inside,' said Aunty Ivy. 'They're in the sitting room, both of them.'

CHAPTER TEN

THERE WAS NO TIME TO REFLECT ON HIS BETRAYAL, no time to think at all. Harry dragged Ocky protesting along the passage and through the scullery to the back door. He remembered the vegetable garden and the sandpit out the back; and the little iron gate that led out to the lane beyond. He'd gone that way often enough with his mother. Blinded by the dark, he blundered into a pile of peasticks. What he tripped over after that he wasn't sure – it sounded like a watering can – but he ended up on his side in the sandpit still holding onto Ocky, his ankle throbbing with pain. When he got to his feet again he found he was able to do little more than hop. He could hear voices from inside the house now. Ocky was trying to pull away from him but he dared not let her go – he'd never find her again in the darkness.

'*Va bene, va bene* Ocky,' he said, stroking her head. 'Don't you worry. I won't let them catch us, I promise I won't. Come on now.'

He found the gate easily enough and was gone down the lane, running and hopping as best he could. By the time they reached the end of the lane his eyes had become more accustomed to the dark. Across the road and up the hill he could see the phone box and beyond it the car outside number twenty-two. Whoever it was in the driver's seat wore a peaked cap and was lighting a cigarette.

'We'll go nice and slow, Ocky,' he said, 'so's no one'll notice us.' He went down towards the Promenade and the beach because it was the only way he knew to go. He had some thoughts of hiding out in a bathing hut perhaps or in one of the boats drawn up on the sand. A few people eyed them from under their umbrellas as they passed by, and Harry knew they were talking about them as he hurried on down towards the Promenade.

The street lamps were lit all the way along and he could see the lights of the pier reflected in the sea beyond. He would go along the beach. No one would see them down there, and maybe they'd find some-where they could hide out.

It was hard work running and hopping in the sand,

and harder still to hold on to Ocky. He tried every door of a line of beach huts, but they were all locked. His ankle tortured him with every step so he was reduced now to a stumbling walk. When he'd gone as far as his ankle could take him he sat down against the sea wall to regain his strength and to ease the pain in his ankle. As he sat there, the rain lashing at him, it came to him at last that there was nowhere to hide any more, that there was nowhere to run to. He wiped the tears and the rain from his face as Ocky climbed onto his lap and began to pull at his oak apple necklace. He prised her fingers off it and picked up a large shell from the sand beside him. 'Mum told me you can hear the sea in one of these,' he said, and he held it to Ocky's ear. 'Hear it, can you?' Ocky took it from him and smelt it. Harry laughed away his tears and hugged her to him. All he could see in front of him was a line of surf and the dark sea beyond. 'That's the only way we could go now,' he said. 'Not much good to us, is it though, is it, Ocky? I can't swim, can I?'

The torchlight and the voices came from the Promenade above them, the torchlight sweeping out over the beach to the water's edge and then moving across the sand towards them. Harry was on his feet and running.

'They've got to be somewhere.' It was Bill's voice. 'They've got to be. She said it was his favourite place. He wouldn't know anywhere else to go. You go down on the beach, Sergeant, and I'll stay up here.'

Crouching, Harry ran along the sea wall. His only chance now was to outrun the beam of the torch. He'd have done it, too, if he hadn't tripped over a rock. Ocky screeched and pulled away as he fell, face forward in the sand, and when he looked up she was scampering along the beach with the torchlight following her. And then out of the blackness, from nowhere it seemed, came two dogs racing across the sand. For a moment Harry lay there and watched as Ocky reached the steps up to the Promenade. He saw her stand up and look behind her almost as if she was waiting for him. Then she was gone, the dogs baying and barking after her.

He ran as fast as his ankle would allow him, hopping up the steps and then setting off down the Promenade after them. He could see her far ahead of him now, a black shadow racing under the lamplights. Behind him he could hear Bill's voice shouting at him to stop. He looked over his shoulder once. Bill could have been either of the two figures running after him along the Promenade. One was ahead of the other and gaining on him. But they did not concern him, not any more.

175

The sound of Ocky's terrified screeching brought fresh power to his legs, and he ran now oblivious of the pain in his ankle. Someone ahead of him, alerted by Bill's shouting, reached out and tried to stop him but he weaved around him and ran on. He saw the dogs swerve off the Promenade and on to the pier – greyhounds they looked like. Ocky was well out of sight by the time Harry reached the pier, but he could tell by the baying of the dogs that they knew where she was. Side by side they raced up the left hand side of the pier and Harry followed them, screaming at them to frighten them off; but he wasn't close enough for them even to hear him.

He never saw the fight. It happened almost at the end of the pier in the darkness between two lamps. He heard it, though – a terrible cacophony of snarling and screeching and wounded whimpering – and at the end of it a splash and then silence. The two dogs came loping into the lamplight, tongues lolling and tails waving.

'No!' cried Harry. 'No!' Behind him he could hear hollow footsteps pounding along the pier. They were closing in on him all the time. Harry thought he knew exactly the spot where the dogs must have caught up with Ocky, but when he reached it and looked out over the rail he could see nothing down in the oil-black sea as it heaved under the pier below him. Then further out and to the right of him he heard a single stifled screech.

That was enough for him. He never thought about it. He climbed through the railings, stood for a moment on the edge, and then jumped. As he fell he heard Bill's cry: 'Don't do it, Harry! Don't!' And then the cold salt sea was in his eyes and his ears and his mouth, and he was fighting upwards to find air. When at last he broke the surface a wave tossed him upwards, sideways and took him down again before he could draw a breath. No matter how hard he kicked and flailed, the sea would not let him have the time to breathe before it covered him again. Once when he came up he caught sight of the pier above him. Several faces were leaning over the rail and shouting down at him, but he could not make out what they were saying before he was dragged down again. He could feel the cold stiffening his legs already, the strength was not there when he kicked. Each time he sank it was taking longer for him to come up. Once he thought he saw Ocky almost within reach and called out to her but the sea filled his mouth before any sound came out and sank him again like a stone.

He thought the moon was falling out of the sky at first and held up his hand to protect his head. Then the moon splashed into the water right beside him and he reached out for it and clung on, coughing the sea out of his lungs.

He felt the rope on the edge of the moon, understood it was a lifebuoy, and knew it would float, that the sea could not drag him down and drown him now, not if he could hold on. He looked around for Ocky. He called for her over and over again. There was shouting above him. He looked up in time to see a man in shirt and trousers standing under the lamp by the railings. He dived in and disappeared. Only when the head came up and shook the water from his hair did he see it was Bill. 'Ocky,' Harry shouted. 'I can't find Ocky.' Bill shouted back at him but Harry could not hear what he was saying.

Bill swam over to him and clung to Harry's lifebuoy. 'You've got to find her!' Harry shouted. 'You've got to. She was over there. Over there!'

'All right, I'll try,' Bill said and he lifted up the lifebuoy and dropped it over Harry's head. 'But you hold on tight, Harry, you hear me? Hold on.' Bill waved up to the pier. Harry watched as another man leapt off the pier, landed in the water a few feet away. 'Look after him,' Bill shouted, and he swam away into the darkness.

Harry could no longer feel himself below his waist. The man had one hand on his lifebuoy now. 'Hang on tight now, son; and keep your mouth closed,' he said. 'We'll have you safe in no time.' And he swam on his back hauling Harry along beside him. Several times they were swamped by waves, but Harry kept his eyes and his mouth closed tight and when each wave passed and he found it hadn't sunk him he worried less about the next one.

In between his puffing and his blowing his rescuer joked as he swam. 'Fine night for a swim,' he said. 'Who'd be a fish, eh?' But with his quips came words of encouragement. 'Not far now, son. Keep your pecker up. Won't be long.' It seemed long enough to Harry, but then he was being washed in through the surf and there were voices around him and hands grabbing his shoulders. He was lifted out of the lifebuoy and carried up the beach. It seemed as if there were a hundred people there. Torches flashed in his face, and then Aunty Ivy was there and organising noisily.

'Give him to me. I'll look after him,' she said.

'We'll need blankets, lots of them. And tea, hot tea.'

'Someone said there's a monkey out there,' said somebody.

'There is,' said Aunty Ivy.

'She's a chimpanzee,' said Harry as they lowered him onto the sand. Aunty Ivy covered him with a coat.

'It's your dad out there, isn't it?' she said.

'Yes,' said Harry, who was beginning to shake convulsively.

'I've got to get you home, pet,' said Aunty Ivy pulling him closer to her. 'I've got to get you warm.'

'No,' said Harry, 'I'm staying.' He looked at Aunty Ivy. 'He jumped in after me and then he went after Ocky. I've got to stay, I've got to.' The determination in his voice deterred any further attempts to persuade him. Aunty Ivy saw to it that he was covered in a heap of coats and blankets and then sat down and waited beside him.

From the pier someone fired a series of Verey lights into the air, each bringing daylight to the beach for a few brief moments. There were people standing knee-deep in the surf shining their torches out to sea.

Harry closed his eyes and prayed. It was a bargaining prayer promising to take Ocky back to Signor Blondini if only God would save her. But more and more he found himself praying not for Ocky but for Bill, and for Bill's safety he promised he'd give up anything God wanted, anything at all, and he promised faithfully he'd never run away again and he'd never skip school, not even once. 'Please God, I'll do anything. You can have anything,' he said it aloud now, 'just don't let them be drowned.' With his head on his arms he rocked back and forth, repeating his promises over and over again. Then someone shouted they could see something and there was a great commotion. Harry looked up. Several of them were running out through the surf, but all it turned out to be was a piece of bobbing flotsam. He prayed again. More Verey lights went up and lit the sky. He could see the little parachutes on them as they fell, but nothing more was seen. A gun boomed in the distance and someone said the lifeboat had been launched.

'Here, pet,' said Aunty Ivy, and she put a mug of tea in his hands. 'Get that down you,' she said. His hands were so numb that at first she had to help him hold it, but with every sip of it the warmth flowed through him, stilled his chattering teeth and brought some feeling back into his fingers. Aunty Ivy put her arm round him and hugged him close.

'It's all my fault, pet,' she said. 'If I hadn't phoned them none of this would have happened. But what else could I do? I had to tell them. They're your own mum and dad. You couldn't stay with me for ever, could you, pet? You had to go home. It's where you belong. And your poor mother, I couldn't bear the thought of her not knowing where you were. When I spoke to her on the phone she was worried sick about you. Don't you know you're the apple of her eye? And Bill, he thinks the world of you, like I do. Why else would he jump in after you, ask yourself that?'

Harry already had. Everything Aunty Ivy was telling him was true except that it was not her fault Bill and Ocky were out there in the sea. It wasn't Aunty Ivy who had run off with Ocky, was it? It was no one's fault but his. 'Dear God,' he prayed silently, 'you can take anything, even my father's medal, even my lucky necklace, but bring them back. Don't let them die.' He'd not thought of the medal until that moment but he was suddenly aware that he could not feel the medal in his trouser pocket. He thought perhaps it was because his legs were so cold, so he reached down under the coats and blankets and felt his pockets, both of them. It was gone, there was no doubt about it.

'Aunty Ivy,' he said. 'I think I've lost it.'

'What, pet?'

'The medal, my father's medal. It must've fallen out in the sea.'

Aunty Ivy's voice was stern as he'd never heard it before. 'Then it's back where it belongs, isn't it, pet?'

Harry looked at her. 'What do you mean?' he said. Aunty Ivy didn't say anything for a moment.

'Your mother told me all about your father, the one that died in the war,' she said, 'how he crashed out there into the sea. Proud of him she was, pet. So all I'm thinking is that if you've lost his medal, then it's probably at the bottom of the sea and that's where it belongs isn't it? After all, when's all said and done, it's his medal, pet, not yours. the war's been over a long time now. It's time to forget it. We've got to get on with living again. And talking of living, pet,' she said, squeezing his shoulder, 'look what I see.' She was pointing down the beach, and Bill walked out of the darkness carrying Ocky in his arms.

'The current took us away from the pier,' he said. 'We were washed up a long way down the beach, weren't we, little fellow?' Ocky whimpered and buried her head in his shoulder. Someone called out that they were both all right, and a Verey light burst immediately overhead. Ocky looked up at it and hooted and blinked and then everyone was running towards them cheering and laughing.

'Is she all right?' Harry asked, standing up and throwing off his pile of coats.

'Bit wet,' said Bill smiling, 'and she swallowed a few mouthfuls of seawater, but she'll be fine. She's feeling a bit sorry for herself of course, and I don't think she likes swimming much.'

'P'raps they can't swim,' Harry said.

'Nor can you,' said Bill, 'but you went in after her.' Ocky seemed to recognise Harry's voice for she began to wriggle and squirm in Bill's arms. 'Here,' said Bill holding her out to him, 'she's yours, isn't she?'

'Not really,' said Harry, and Ocky put her arms round his neck and clung to him. 'She belongs to someone else really, Signor Blondini at the circus.'

'Then we'd better take her back to him, don't you think?' Bill said.

'Do you think he's missed her?' Harry asked.

'More than you know, Harry,' he said, wiping his face with a blanket someone had wrapped around his shoulders. 'But no more than we've all missed you, Harry. Let's take you home.'

'No one's going anywhere,' said Aunty Ivy firmly, 'not until I say so, and I say you're all coming back with me and you'll all have a nice hot bath. Then you can dry off in front of the fire and have a cup of cocoa, and *then* you can go home.' No one argued with her.

As the police car drove away from the terrace in the dark hours of the early morning Bill vowed he would never ever have a bath with a chimpanzee again. 'If she wasn't pulling the plug out,' he said, 'she was chasing the soap around the bath. And then all she did when she caught it was throw it at you.'

Ocky played with her feet for a bit and then curled

up beside Harry on the back seat and fell asleep. Bill and the policeman who was driving (he was the one who had rescued Harry) exchanged cheerful banter about the outsize clothes they'd both had to borrow. Harry leaned up against Bill's shoulder and felt his arm come around him. He was too tired to worry even about facing the music when he got home and he was drifting into welcome sleep when the policeman spoke again.

'Asleep, is he, sir?'

'I think so,' said Bill.

'I was telling them back at the station, sir, in Bournemouth, when I went to change; I was telling them that's how we like to breed them in London. Took some pluck that, sir, your lad jumping into the sea after the chimp. I know he's led us a right dance but I'm telling you you're a lucky man, sir, having a son like that.'

'I know I am,' said Bill. 'There's not another one like him, that's for sure.'

'I should hope not, sir. We don't want to be jumping off piers every night, do we?' And Harry was asleep before they'd finished laughing.

It was dawn when he woke. Ocky was still asleep snoring on the seat beside him. Bill was shaking his shoulder. 'We're here, Harry,' said Bill as the car slowed to a stop. Harry sat up and looked out of the window. He did not recognise it until he saw the sign over the gate: 'Blondini's Circus'.

'I thought we'd better get this over before we went home,' said Bill. 'What do you think?' Harry did not have to ask what he meant. 'We won't be more than a few minutes,' Bill told the policeman. Ocky woke easily enough but Harry was still only half awake when they got out into the cold morning air.

No one was about except for a postman plodding wearily along the pavement towards them, a sack over his shoulder. When he saw Ocky he stopped, stared and then crossed over onto the other side of the road. Bill took Harry's hand and they walked through the entrance towards a semi-circle of caravans drawn up beyond the huge circus marquee. There was a strong smell of straw and dung, a smell that brought back memories to Harry of his night at the circus – it seemed like a year ago now.

Ocky was wide awake, pulling hard on Harry's hand. She knew where she was going now and was gathering speed all the time. In the end Harry could hold her no longer and she broke free, scampering away on all fours towards a yellow caravan; it was the only one with smoke coming out of its chimney. At the top of the steps she reached for the door handle, opened it and disappeared. They could hear her hooting inside. Harry hesitated for a moment.

'Do I have to?' he said.

'I think so, Harry, don't you?' said Bill. And they climbed the steps together and went in.

Signor Blondini was sitting in an armchair by an unmade bed. Ocky was standing on his lap and Signor Blondini was fending her off, the tears running down his cheeks.

'It's me,' said Harry.

Signor Blondini seemed uncertain at first. His brow furrowed straining to see who it was. Then he smiled and nodded. 'Ah, it's you. It's the bambino,' he said. 'The bambino from the park, eh?'

'That's where I found her,' Harry said. 'I didn't mean to steal her, honest I didn't. I just wanted to borrow her for a bit.'

Signor Blondini beckoned him closer. Harry felt Bill's hand in the small of his back pushing him forward. 'You like her, eh bambino? You like my Ocky that much?' he said, and he reached out and took Harry's hand in his.

'Yes.'

'And you looked after her good?'

'Yes.'

'He knows what he did wasn't right, Signor

Blondini,' said Bill, 'but he did save her life. He jumped into the sea after her. He saved her from drowning.'

Signor Blondini was trying to calm Ocky. He stroked her on her head and tickled her behind her ears. '*Va bene*, Ocky. *Va bene*,' he said; and Ocky settled down on his lap and pulled at his braces. Signor Blondini wiped his eyes with his handkerchief and then he looked up at Harry, yet not *at* him, not exactly. Harry had seen those eyes before somewhere but he could not think where. They belonged to someone else, he was sure of it. They were dull and seemed not to focus on him but looked through him or past him. And then he noticed the costume hanging over the back of a chair, a black costume with large red and gold butterflies all over it; and beside it was a black and battered violin case and on top of that lay a wig, a wig of long red hair.

'You're that clown, aren't you?' said Harry. 'You're Mr Nobody, aren't you?'

And Signor Blondini smiled and nodded. 'Don't you tell no one, bambino,' he said. 'It's a big secret. But you're right. When I put that costume on, I'm Mr Nobody, Mr Nobody the Clown.' He patted Ocky's head. 'And this is not just a chimpanzee, bambino, not to Mr Nobody. She's Mr Nobody's eyes. Mr Nobody, he don't see so good no more; and Ocky, she guides him where he wants to go. She leads him around the ring so he don't fall over. She's his *occhi*. And you want to know what *occhi* means, bambino? It means "eyes" in Italiano. You understand now, eh? And I tell you, Mr Nobody, he don't care that you borrowed his Ocky, bambino; all he cares about is that you brought him back his eyes so that he can do his act like he always did all his life, like he wants to do till the day he dies.' A dog barked outside and Ocky sat up and stiffened. '*Va bene, va bene*, Ocky,' said Signor Blondini softly, and Ocky seemed to forget about the dog almost at once.

'"*Va bene*", what does it mean?' Harry asked.

'*Va bene*? It means it's all right, bambino. It means everything's going to be all right now,' said Signor Blondini.

Back home, once the tears and the hugging were over, they sat down together to a breakfast of tea and Granny Wesley's lumpy porridge. In between the mouthfuls Harry told them everything, everything he thought they needed to know anyway.

After Georgie had finished feeding, his mother held him out to Harry and Harry took him, one arm behind the head to support it, and then laid him over his shoulder and burped him expertly.

'Where on earth did you learn to do that?' his

mother asked. That was a part of the story he'd left out. He gave Georgie back without answering and ran upstairs to change into his school clothes. When he came down again they were all talking together in the kitchen. They fell silent as he came in.

'I've got something for Georgie,' he said, giving his mother the oak apple necklace. 'You can keep it for him till he's older.' They looked blankly at him. 'It's for good luck,' he said, and he turned to go.

'Where do you think you're going?' Bill asked. 'You've hardly slept more than a couple of hours all night.'

'School,' Harry said. 'It's Monday, isn't it? I'm going to school. I mustn't skip a single day, not any more. I promised someone.'

Which type of book do you like best?

Take the quiz . . . then read the book!

Who would you like to have an adventure with?
a) On my own
b) A ghost
c) Someone in my family
d) My best friend
e) My pet

Where would you like to go on holiday?
a) A remote island or a far-away mountain
b) A fantasy world
c) Anywhere as long as my family and friends are there
d) A different time period
e) The countryside

I would like to be . . .
a) Explorer
b) Author
c) Someone who helps others
d) Warrior
e) Circus ringmaster

My favourite stories are . . .
a) Full of adventure
b) Magical
c) About friendships and family
d) War stories
e) About animals

If you answered mostly with A you'll enjoy . . .

KENSUKE'S KINGDOM

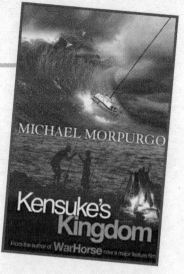

Washed up on an island
with no food and water,
Michael cannot survive.
But he is not alone . . .

If you answered mostly with B you'll enjoy . . .

THE GHOST OF GRANIA O'MALLEY

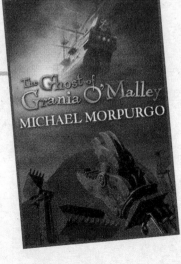

There is gold in the Big
Hill, but Jessie and Jake
can't bear for the hill to be
destroyed. Can they save
it before it's too late?

If you answered mostly with C you'll enjoy . . .

LONG WAY HOME

George doesn't want to spend his summer with another foster family . . . but this time he may have found somewhere to call home.

If you answered mostly with D you'll enjoy . . .

FRIEND OR FOE

It is the Blitz. One night David and his friend see a German plane crash on the moors. Do they leave the airmen to die?

If you answered mostly with E you'll enjoy . . .

WAR HORSE

In the deadly chaos of the
First World War, one horse
witnesses the reality of
battle from both sides
of the trenches.

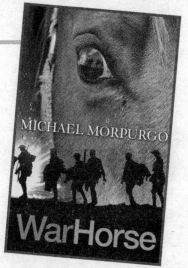

MICHAEL MORPURGO
The master storyteller